Alfred Hitchcock and
The Three Investigators

in

The Secret of
Phantom Lake

Text by William Arden

Based on characters created by Robert Arthur

D1486074

Armada

First published in the U.K. in 1974 by
William Collins Sons & Co. Ltd., London and Glasgow.
This edition was first published in 1976 by
William Collins Sons & Co. Ltd.,
14 St. James's Place, London SW1A 1PF.

Printed in Great Britain by
Love & Malcomson Ltd., Brighton Road,
Redhill, Surrey.

Contents

A Message from Alfred Hitchcock

An ancient shipwreck! A pirate hoard! A ghost town! An island of phantoms! Confound that rascally juvenile confidence man, Jupiter Jones! How can I resist announcing this tale with such tantalizing elements in it?

So once more I take up my pen to invite all adventurous readers to join me. But step carefully, and look behind you—mystery and danger await all who follow The Three Investigators to Phantom Lake!

For the deprived few who live in regions so remote that they are still ignorant of our trio, be informed that their annoyingly brainy leader is the overweight Jupiter Jones. Peter Crenshaw is the tall, muscular Second Investigator, and Bob Andrews is the small, but dogged, Research man.

Residents of Rocky Beach, California—a town a few miles north of Hollywood—they made their headquarters in a hidden mobile home trailer in The Jones Salvage Yard, owned by Jupiter's aunt and uncle. From this hideaway they sally forth to foil the most clever villains and unravel the darkest of riddles.

But now comes a riddle more than a hundred years old! Can even our formidable trio solve it? What is the secret locked in a yellowing letter and a long-lost sailor's journal? Was a hoard of pirate treasure spirited from a sinking ship one stormy night long ago, and who are the shadowy men lurking in the path of the boys?

Can the stubborn trio solve a message from the dead, and find the secret of Phantom Lake? And if they do— can they find it in time?

We shall see!

ALFRED HITCHCOCK

I

The Sea Chest

"Wow!" Bob Andrews cried. "It's a real Malay kris!"

Eyes shining, Bob displayed the rippled blade of the long knife to his two companions, Jupiter Jones and Pete Crenshaw. The boys were in a roadside museum a few miles north of their home in Rocky Beach. Pete gently felt the wavy edge of the kris and shuddered. Jupiter nodded wisely.

"Many ships sailed from California to the East Indies in the old days," Jupiter remarked. "A number of the artifacts in this little museum came from the Orient." Pete and Bob groaned silently as Jupe began to lecture them. The stocky boy had a head full of interesting facts, but he tended to become unbearably pompous when sharing his knowledge.

Aunt Mathilda Jones interrupted the lecture by calling across the room, "I'm more interested now in where these artifacts are going, Jupiter Jones! Stop loafing, you young scamps, and load the truck."

"Yes, Aunt Mathilda," Jupiter said meekly.

The tourist museum, which specialised in relics from old seafaring days, was closing down. Aunt

9

Mathilda and Uncle Titus Jones had arranged to buy its small collection for resale in The Jones Salvage Yard, the most elegant junkyard on the West Coast.

Aunt Mathilda really ran the salvage yard, as Uncle Titus was more interested in scouting for exciting new junk. A large, powerful, rather sharp-tongued woman, she was basically good-natured and kind. But when she saw boys around, she had only one idea: put them to work! Jupiter, who lived with his uncle and aunt, tried to keep out of Aunt Mathilda's way. He and his two friends had their own important business to attend to—running their junior detective firm, The Three Investigators. But this morning Aunt Mathilda had spotted the boys in the junkyard and demanded their help. On the very first day of Christmas vacation, they were trapped!

Sighing, the boys began to carry items outside to Hans, one of the two big Bavarian brothers who worked at the salvage yard. Noting the boys' expressions, Hans mischievously started to whistle "Jingle Bells" as he loaded the yard's pickup truck. Aunt Mathilda watched the boys for a moment, then returned to taking inventory with the museum's owner, Mr Acres.

When the inventory was finished, Aunt Mathilda went to help the boys pack some boxes at the back of the exhibition room. Mr Acres went to the entrance hall to tend to a visitor who had just come in. Moments later, the boys and Aunt Mathilda heard a voice shouting at Mr Acres.

"I don't care who you promised it to!"

Mr Acres's voice was soothing. "Please now, sir—"

"It's mine," the angry voice cried, "and I want it now!"

The voice was hoarse and rasping with a menacing edge. Aunt Mathilda hurried towards the entrance hall with the boys behind her. As they reached Mr Acres, he was saying,

"I'm sorry, but I've sold everything in the museum to The Jones Salvage Yard. No exceptions."

Mr Acres was standing over an ornate Oriental teakwood chest bound with heavily decorated brass.

Facing the owner across the chest was a short man with a full black beard. His glittering dark eyes were set deep in a weather-wrinkled, sunburned face. Two long scars ran down his cheek into the beard. He wore a heavy, sailor's pea-jacket, dark blue bell-bottom trousers, and a merchant sailor's cap with faded brass braid.

The short stranger glared at Mr Acres and snarled, "*I'm* making an exception, you hear me? The chest belongs to me, and I aim to have it back. I'm warning you—!"

Mr Acres bristled. "Now you listen to me, my man! I—!"

"The name's Jim," the stranger growled. "Java Jim, they call me, and I brought that chest a long crûise. There's danger in that chest, you hear?"

The boys gulped. Java Jim turned his glittering eyes on them and muttered an oath.

"What do you brats want, eh?" he snarled. "Sail off now, you hear? The old lady there, too. Shove away!"

Jupiter looked quickly at Aunt Mathilda and suppressed a grin. Aunt Mathilda's face was turning beetroot red.

"What!" Aunt Mathilda roared at the sailor. "What did you say to me, you bearded clown! If I wasn't a lady I'd throw you out of here myself!"

Stunned by Aunt Mathilda's fury, the sailor fell back with the large woman following him.

"It seems you've made an error, Mr Java Jim," said Mr Acres with a smile. "This lady happens to own The Jones Salvage Yard. The chest you want belongs to her now."

Java Jim blinked. "I . . . Well, I'm right sorry, ma'am. It's just my hot temper, I do apologise, no offence meant. Been on ships too long, round just men, eh? And now that I've found my chest, I just lost my head."

All the violent anger seemed to have gone out of the bearded man. Aunt Mathilda calmed down as quickly as she had exploded. She nodded at the Oriental chest, which the three boys were now examining.

"If that chest belongs to you, how did it get here?" Aunt Mathilda asked.

"Stolen, ma'am," Java Jim replied promptly. "Some scoundrel stole it right off my ship two weeks ago when we hit port up in San Francisco. Sold it to a secondhand dealer on the waterfront up there. But the dealer had sent it down here before I got to him, so I came after it."

"Well . . ." Aunt Mathilda began slowly.

Bob, who had the chest open now, pointed to the inside of the raised lid. "There's a name on the lid—*Argyll Queen*. Was that the name of your ship, Mr Java?"

"No, boy," Java Jim said. "It's an old chest, probably been through fifty hands over the years. That name was in it when I bought it in Singapore."

Mr Acres said, "I did get it just yesterday from Walt Baskins in San Francisco, Mrs Jones. I had a standing order with him for any items of local interest for the museum. I forgot to cancel the order when I decided to sell out."

"I'm ready to pay a fair price," Java Jim said quickly.

"Well," Aunt Mathilda said again, "I suppose it belongs to you. You can pay what it cost Mr Acres, and—"

A sudden whirring sound filled the museum.

"What—?" Bob began, and looked up from the old chest.

There was a sharp click.

A flash in the light—and a short, wicked dagger whizzed past Jupiter's ear and buried itself in the wall!

2

Danger Past and Present

FOR A LONG moment everyone froze. The dagger quivered in the wall.

Then Aunt Mathilda hurried to Jupiter.

"Are you all right, Jupiter?" she cried.

Jupe nodded but sat down weakly on an old bench. The dagger had missed his ear by inches!

"Who threw it?" Mr Acres cried, glancing wildly round.

Java Jim said, "Don't go looking at me!"

"N-n-no one threw it," Bob stammered. "It came out of the chest!"

Mr Acres went over to the chest and looked inside. "Good heavens!" he said. "There's a secret compartment in the bottom! It's open now! Bob must have touched some hidden mechanism that opened it."

"The dagger must have been inside the secret compartment," Bob continued, "on a spring that released when the compartment was opened! A booby trap!"

"To stab anyone who found the hiding place!" Pete exclaimed.

Aunt Mathilda strode towards Java Jim. "If this was your work, I'll have you—!"

"I don't know anything about any booby trap!" the bearded sailor declared angrily.

"No," Jupiter said suddenly. The colour was back in his face now. He pulled the dagger out of the wall and studied the deadly weapon. "It's an Oriental dagger, probably East Indian. I'll bet that booby trap was set a hundred years ago by East Indian pirates!"

"Wow!" Pete said.

"Pirates?" Bob cried.

His eyes sparkling, Jupiter carried the old dagger to the chest and bent down to examine the spring mechanism inside the secret compartment. He nodded triumphantly.

"See! The spring and catch are handmade and rusty," the stocky boy said. "Definitely old work. This is a typical East Indian booby trap to protect hidden valuables. Perhaps the work of Javanese or Malayan pirates!"

"Java like in Java Jim!"

Everyone looked at the bearded sailor again.

"Hold on now," Java Jim said. "It's just a nickname I got when I was young because I lived in Java awhile. I don't know anything about any pirates!"

Pete groaned. "I don't even know where Java is."

"It's a big island in Indonesia," Jupiter explained. "Along with Sumatra and New Guinea and Borneo and Celebes and several thousand smaller islands. Indonesia is an independent country now, but in the old days it was a colony, the Dutch

East Indies. It used to be full of hundreds of little kingdoms called sultanates, ruled by local sultans who were mostly pirates!"

"You mean like Blackbeard?" Pete asked. "Sailing ships, and cannons, and the skull-and-crossbones and all that?"

"Not exactly, Pete," Jupiter answered a trifle pompously. "Those were the hallmarks of Western pirates. Blackbeard was English, you know. The East Indian pirates had no big ships or Jolly Roger flags, and few cannon. They were natives who lurked in hundreds of East Indian islands—in small rivers and villages—and attacked European and American ships by boarding them in swarms.

"The Western ships were there to get pepper and other spices, and tin, and tea and silks from China. Our ships carried manufactured goods for trading and also many bags of gold and silver for purchasing Oriental products. The East Indian pirates attacked the sailing ships to steal money and weapons. Sometimes our ships would retaliate and attack the pirates in their lairs. The pirates had all kinds of defence tricks, including booby traps in chests."

Bob said, "You mean our sailors would try to steal back what the pirates stole? You think this booby trap comes from way back then, Jupe?"

"I'm certain of it, Bob. Although," he added thoughtfully, "they do say that there are small bands of pirates still hidden in the remote islands."

"Jupe, look!" Pete cried. The tall boy had been

rummaging in the old chest. Now he held up a small, shiny object. "A ring! It was in the secret compartment!"

"Is there anything else?" Bob exclaimed.

Java Jim pushed Pete aside and bent over the chest. "Let's see! No, curse the luck, nothing else!"

Jupiter took the ring from Pete. It was intricately carved in what could have been gold or brass. The design was Oriental, and a red stone gleamed in the centre.

"Is it real, Jupe?" asked Pete.

"I don't know, Pete. It could be. They had a lot of real gold and jewels in the Indies. But they had a lot of fake stuff, too. Trinkets traded by Europeans to natives who couldn't tell the difference."

Java Jim reached out for the ring.

"Real or fake, boy, the ring's mine, eh? The chest was stolen from me, and everything in it is mine," the bearded sailor said. "Name your price, I'll take my chest."

"Well, let me see," Aunt Mathilda began.

Jupiter spoke quickly, "We don't *know* the chest is his, Aunt Mathilda. His name isn't on it, and all we have is his story."

"You calling me a liar, boy?" Java Jim growled.

"Show us a bill of sale," Jupiter said stoutly, "or some witnesses who saw you buy it, or knew you had it on your ship."

"All my shipmates saw the chest! Now you—"

"Then," Jupiter said firmly, "I suggest we hold the chest at the salvage yard, and promise not to sell it for a week while you bring proof. I'm sure you can wait a few days."

"That sounds fair to me," Mr Acres said.

Java Jim glared. "Blast you, I've had enough! I'm taking what's mine, and don't try to stop me!" He advanced on Jupiter, his hoarse voice threatening. "First I want that ring, boy. Hand it over."

As the sailor closed in on him, Jupiter backed towards the outside doorway.

"Now look here you—!" cried Aunt Mathilda.

"Shut up, curse you!" Java Jim snapped.

A large shadow appeared in the open doorway. Hans, the big, blond helper at the salvage yard, came into the museum.

"You will not talk so to Aunt Mathilda," Hans said. "You will apologise, yes."

"He's trying to take a ring from Jupiter and steal that chest, Hans!" Bob cried.

"Get him, Hans!" ordered Jupe.

"I get him," Hans said, and lunged forward.

With another oath, Java Jim flung Mr Acres into Hans's path and ran to the back of the museum.

"After him!" Pete yelled.

But Hans stumbled over Mr Acres and careered into the boys. By the time they had all untangled themselves, Java Jim had escaped out of the back door. A car started somewhere behind the museum. When the boys ran outside, all they saw was a cloud of dust where the car had vanished up the coast highway and round a steep hill.

"And good riddance," Aunt Mathilda said. "Now we can finish loading the truck."

"Gosh," Bob said, "I wonder why he wanted that chest?"

"Just trying to steal a good chest, I'm sure," Aunt Mathilda said. "Get to work, boys. We'll need another trip as it is."

An hour later the truck was loaded as full as it could be, and Hans and Aunt Mathilda got into the cab. Mr Acres helped the boys climb into the back. Jupiter was frowning.

"Mr Acres," the stocky leader of the trio said slowly, "you said that the dealer in San Francisco, Mr Baskins, sent you that chest because it was of local interest?"

"That's right, Jupiter," Mr Acres said. "That name in it, *Argyll Queen*, is the name of a ship that sank just off Rocky Beach about a hundred years ago. Small items sometimes turn up from the ship, and I display them."

"Of course," Jupiter said. "That big square-rigger that hit a reef in 1870. I remember now."

The truck drove off, and the boys settled down in the back. Jupiter seemed lost in thought, so Bob and Pete talked and looked at the scenery. Then Pete began to frown. As the truck drove into the salvage yard, he leaned close to Jupiter.

"Jupe! I think someone followed us! A green Volkswagen was behind us all the way, and it just came into our street!"

The boys jumped from the truck and hurried to the front gate of the yard. A green VW *was* parked across the street. But before the boys could see who was in it, the small car suddenly drove off with squealing tyres.

"Gosh," Pete said. "You think it was that Java Jim?"

"Perhaps," Jupiter said. "But he escaped from the museum in the other direction, Pete."

"Maybe someone else wants that old chest," Bob said.

"Or is interested in the wreck of the *Argyll Queen*," Jupiter said. His eyes were bright as he sensed a mystery. "This could be a case for The Three Investigators! We'll—"

"So there you are!" Aunt Mathilda appeared behind the boys. "That truck won't unload itself. Get to work, boys."

Sheepishly, the three boys returned to the truck and began to unload it. The mystery of the old chest would have to wait!

3

The Wreck of the "Argyll Queen"

IT WAS NOON before the truck was unloaded. Aunt Mathilda went across the street to the Jones house to prepare lunch. The boys hurried at once to the old chest.

"We'll study it in Headquarters," Jupiter said. "You two carry it. There's something I have to do first."

The stout boy ran ahead, leaving Bob and Pete standing over the big, heavy chest. With sighs of protest, Pete picked up one end and Bob the other. They struggled over to Jupe's outdoor workshop in a corner of the junkyard. Beneath the workbench began Tunnel Two, a large galvanised pipe that ran back under a mountain of junk—to the secret headquarters of The Three Investigators!

Headquarters was an old, damaged mobile home trailer that the boys had fixed up. Outside, it was hidden from sight by carefully placed stacks of junk. Inside was a modern office, complete with darkroom, lab, desk, typewriter, tape recorder, and telephone. There was a periscope for seeing out over the surrounding junk, and all sorts of special detective equipment, mostly of Jupiter's invention.

But one of Headquarters' cleverest features was also a big drawback, as Bob and Pete now realised when they lugged the old chest up to Tunnel Two.

"It's too big to get into the tunnel!" Pete groaned.

The boys set down the chest and looked at each other.

"We made all the entrances just big enough for us," Bob pointed out glumly. "I bet it won't fit any of them!"

Just then Jupiter came crawling out of Tunnel Two, looking excited. Bob and Pete blurted out their problem.

"Hmmmmmm," Jupiter said, eyeing the narrow entrance of Tunnel Two. "I should have thought of that. Maybe we can get it inside through Easy Three."

Easy Three was the simplest entrance to the trailer. A big oak door, still in its frame, leaned against some timber. A rusty key, concealed in a barrel of other rusty objects, opened the door, and a short passageway led to the original side door of the trailer.

"We'd better measure the trailer door first," said Bob.

"And we'll have to wait until no one else is in the yard before using Easy Three," Jupiter added. "Meanwhile, men, I've just found out that Java Jim's whole story was a lie!"

"Gee, Jupe," Pete said, "how could you know that?"

"I called the secondhand dealer in San Francisco,

Mr Baskins," Jupiter told them. "He didn't get the chest from a sailor, he got it from another secondhand shop in Santa Barbara! The other dealer got it from a lady six months ago!"

"Wow!" Pete said. "Maybe Java Jim's not even a sailor!"

"A good point," Jupiter agreed seriously. "Java Jim could be wearing the pea-jacket and bell-bottoms as a disguise, to fool us into thinking he's a sailor. Not a very good disguise, either. Those clothes are too heavy for Southern California, even in December."

"Java couldn't have known he'd run into *us*, Jupe," Bob objected, "and mornings and nights are cold around Christmas."

"That's true, I guess," Jupiter conceded. "Anyway, Java Jim *was* at Mr Baskins's shop yesterday —only he told an entirely different story! He said his sister had sold the chest while he was away, and he wanted to get it back!"

Pete was puzzled. "Why change his story?"

"Probably because he thought his new story would make us give him the chest faster, and because he doesn't want anyone to guess his real reason for wanting the chest," Jupiter reasoned. "But his story to Mr Baskins proves one thing— Java Jim knew a woman had sold the chest six months ago! Only he couldn't have learned that until recently, or he'd have traced the chest sooner."

"Gosh," Bob said, "why does he want it so much? I mean, it's just an empty chest."

"Except for that ring," Pete said. "Maybe it's valuable."

"But it's just one ring, and Java didn't even know it was there until we found the secret compartment," Bob pointed out.

"Maybe he knew *something* was in the chest," Pete suggested.

"Or perhaps," Jupiter said, "the chest is important because it came from the *Argyll Queen*! Perhaps even from the shipwreck!"

Jupiter's eyes had a special gleam in them—a gleam that meant he was at work on a mystery!

"You think Java Jim's interested in a ship that sank over a hundred years ago, Jupe?" Bob said doubtfully.

"But why?" Pete asked.

"I don't know," Jupiter admitted, "but listen! Except for the hidden ring and dagger, the ship's name is all that the chest contains. I think we should investigate the history of the *Argyll Queen*."

"The Historical Society should have something," Bob said.

Pete was unhappy. "I've got to go Christmas shopping with my mother today, and work at home with my dad."

"And I have to go back with the truck for a second load from the museum," Jupiter said. "I guess it's up to you, Bob."

"Fine with me," agreed Bob. He usually handled the team's special research anyway.

Soon after, the boys heard Aunt Mathilda

calling Jupiter, and they split up for lunch.

After lunch, Bob's mother sent him for an extra set of Christmas lights, and it was past three o'clock when he cycled up to the Rocky Beach Historical Society. Inside, a grey-haired lady smiled at him from behind a desk.

"The *Argyll Queen*, young man? Why, yes. I believe we have considerable material on that. A terrible wreck that caused a big stir several years later. Rumours of treasure, you know."

"Treasure?" Bob exclaimed.

"Gold and jewels and all that." The lady smiled. "I don't think much came of it. I'll get you the material, young man."

Bob waited in the central room of the Historical Society with growing excitement. When the grey-haired lady returned, she was carrying a large, hinged file box.

"I'm afraid the material is unorganised," she said.

Bob took the box and hurried into one of the small reading rooms. Alone in the room, he sat at a long table and opened the box.

He blinked in dismay. The box was crammed with papers, pamphlets, small books, and news-paper and magazine articles. There seemed to be no order to the papers at all. With a sigh, he picked up the first article, and a voice spoke above him,

"I'm afraid it'll take days to read all that."

Startled, Bob looked up and saw a small man in an old-fashioned black suit with a waistcoat and gold watch chain. The man had a round, pink face and rimless glasses. He stood smiling down at Bob. His voice was deep but friendly.

"I'm Professor Shay of the Historical Society," the small man said. "Mrs Rutherford told me of your interest in the *Argyll Queen* shipwreck. We like to encourage young people's interest in our work. Perhaps I can save you a lot of reading if you just want a few facts."

"You know about the *Argyll Queen*, sir?" Bob asked.

"It's not my field," Professor Shay admitted, "and I've not been here long, but one of our men is writing a pamphlet on the complete story. I've picked up a lot. Just how much do you know, young man?"

"I know the *Argyll Queen* was a big square-rigger that sank off Rocky Beach in 1870," Bob said promptly, "and there were rumours of treasure on it!"

The professor laughed. "There are rumours of treasure aboard every ship that ever went down, my boy. But you're right about the date." The professor sat down across from Bob. "The *Argyll Queen* was a three-masted, full-rigged ship from Glasgow, Scotland, in the East Indies spice and tin trade. She had put in at San Francisco, and was sailing south for Cape Horn and the trip back to Scotland, when a storm blew her off course. She struck a reef close to shore one night in December 1870.

"It was a terrible storm, and there were few

survivors. Most of her crew tried to get to shore at once and were lost. By sheer chance she didn't sink immediately. The few who did survive were those who remained aboard until dawn, including the Captain, who of course stayed until the last."

"But there wasn't any treasure?"

"I doubt it, young man," Professor Shay said. "The *Queen* went down in relatively shallow water, and divers searched it at the time, and many times afterwards. Even today people occasionally dive down to the wreck after treasure. But all that's ever been found are a few ordinary coins of the period." The professor shook his head. "No, I'm afraid the rumours got started because of another tragedy soon after that seemed to be connected to the *Argyll Queen*."

"Another tragedy, sir?" Bob exclaimed. "What was that?"

"One survivor, a Scottish sailor named Angus Gunn, settled not far from Rocky Beach. In 1872 he was murdered by four men. All four murderers were killed by a posse before they could tell why they had done it. But one of the four was the Captain of the *Argyll Queen*, so people were sure the Captain was after something Gunn had taken from the ship—perhaps treasure, you see? People searched the ship, the shore, and every inch of Gunn's land for years and years, but nothing was ever found.

"Angus Gunn, like many sailors, kept a journal. As a matter of fact, his descendants recently gave the journal to the Society to help with the pamphlet. It was read by the sheriff in 1872, and the Gunn family has searched it ever since, for any hint of treasure—but to no avail. If there was a treasure, and Gunn had it, he left no clues to it in his journal."

Bob frowned. "Was the treasure supposed to be something from the East Indies, where the ship had been, sir?"

"Why, yes, that was the rumour. A pirate hoard. Why? Do you know something, my boy?"

"Er, no, sir," Bob stammered. "I just wondered."

"I see." Professor Shay smiled. "Just why *are* you interested in the *Argyll Queen*, may I ask?"

"We . . . we just are, sir. For a . . . a school project over the Christmas vacation," Bob said lamely.

"Of course," Professor Shay said. "Most commendable, my boy."

"Sir? Could I see the journal and the new pamphlet?"

Professor Shay's eyes seemed to twinkle behind his rimless glasses. "For your school project, eh? Of course, my boy, and if you happen to discover anything new, we'll put your name in our pamphlet."

The professor went away grinning. A few minutes later, Mrs Rutherford brought in a thin manuscript—*Wreck of the Argyll Queen*—and an oilskin-wrapped notebook. Bob began to read them.

It was dusk as Bob cycled up to the back of The Jones Salvage Yard. Round the yard was an unusually colourful fence; it had been decorated by artists of Rocky Beach with an assortment of vivid scenes. Covering the whole back fence was a magnificent painting of the San Francisco fire of 1906.

Bob rode along beside the back fence and stopped about fifty feet from the corner. Here a little dog had been painted into the fire scene, looking sadly up at the flames burning his home. The Investigators had named the dog Rover. Bob picked out the knot hole that formed one of Rover's eyes, reached in, and undid a catch. Three boards in the fence swung up, and he wheeled his bike inside. This was Red Gate Rover, one of the boys' private entrances to the salvage yard.

From here Bob could go directly to Headquarters by crawling through a long, hidden passageway in the junk. But he decided to look into the workshop first. Wheeling his bike to the front of the yard, he spied Pete coming in through the main gate.

" My dad worked me all afternoon," Pete groaned. "Some vacation! I'd almost rather go to school."

The two boys went on to the outdoor workshop. Rounding the piles of junk that defined the workshop area—and kept it from view of the rest of the year—they found Jupiter. He had a light on over the workbench and was studying the Oriental chest. As Bob started to tell what he had learned at the Historical Society, Jupiter waved his hand.

"Wait a minute," the stout leader interrupted, his voice excited. "I've been examining the chest again. Look what I found!"

Jupiter held up an oilskin-wrapped book that looked just like the journal Bob had read at the Historical Society, but thinner. Bob reached out for the book.

A hoarse voice suddenly rasped from the entrance to the workshop area.

"I'll take that book!"

Java Jim stood glaring at the boys.

4

The Second Journal

JUPITER JUMPED up and backed against the stacks of junk. Pete and Bob seemed frozen where they stood.

Java Jim advanced menacingly towards Jupiter, who clutched the oilskin-wrapped book tightly against his shirt.

"Pete!" Jupiter cried. "Plan One!"

Java Jim whirled on Pete and Bob, his dark eyes snapping in his weatherbeaten face. "No tricks now, you kids! I'm warning you."

The bearded sailor's hard stare seemed to bore through Pete and Bob. He watched them a moment, as if daring them to move. Both boys gulped. Java Jim smiled nastily, and turned back to Jupiter.

"Now I'll take the book, boy," Java Jim said hoarsely.

"You're a liar and a thief!" Jupiter cried as he backed away in a circle.

Java Jim laughed. "A thief, am I? Maybe I'm a lot worse, boy, and you think about that! I want that book."

Jupiter kept edging away, drawing the sailor after him until the man was near one particular towering pile of junk, with his back turned to it. Pete and Bob edged along behind Java Jim.

"Now, guys!" Jupiter shouted.

Bob and Pete bent quickly and pulled two long boards from the junk tower behind the sailor. With a curse, Java Jim turned—too late!

"Ahhhhgggggghhh!"

As Bob and Pete leaped out of the way, the wall of junk came crashing down on Java Jim! Boards and bed springs and broken chairs and rolls of ragged rugs fell all over him. The bearded sailor kicked and flailed, trying to protect himself and escape at the same time.

Bob and Pete grinned at the sight, but Jupiter didn't pause.

"Run, men!" the leader yelled.

Stumbling over some of the scattered junk, the three boys ran out of the workshop towards the salvage yard office, where Hans was taking a last item off the truck. They could hear Java Jim still raging and struggling behind them.

"Hans!" Pete cried. "That Java Jim's in the yard! He attacked us!"

"So?" the big Bavarian said. "Come, we will see."

They started back across the salvage yard towards the workshop. The sounds of clattering junk and thrashing had stopped. In the twilight, a small, dark figure dashed from the workshop area towards the back fence of the yard.

"There he goes!" Pete yelled.

Bob cried, "He's carrying something! The

notebook! Jupe, you must have dropped it!"

"Oh, no!" Pete groaned.

Hans said as they ran, "We catch him at the fence, boys."

"I don't think we will," Jupiter panted. "Look, he s at Red Gate Rover! He must have seen one of you come in that way."

"He's through the fence," Bob wailed.

The pursuers ran even faster. But by the time they all piled through Red Gate Rover and stood out on the street, Java Jim was nowhere in sight!

"The green VW!" Pete pointed.

The small green car was driving along the dimly lit street, picking up speed as it turned the corner.

"He's escaped!" Bob moaned.

"I am sorry, boys," Hans said, "but you are all safe. Now I must return to my work. It is almost dinnertime."

The boys went back to the workshop and glumly surveyed the mess their trap had made.

"Now we'll have to pile it all up again," Pete said unhappily, "and we didn't even stop Java Jim. He got away with the book."

"He got away," Jupiter agreed, "but not with the book!"

Smiling, the First Investigator reached inside his shirt and pulled out a thin sheaf of folded papers. It was the notebook—minus its cover!

"The pages were already coming loose from the binding when I discovered the notebook," Jupe explained with a grin. "When I yelled 'Plan One' and Java Jim turned to look at you two, I just

B

pulled the pages out and slipped them in my shirt. Then when we ran, I dropped the cover where Java Jim could see it. The cover and its oilskin wrapping were thick enough together to pass for the whole notebook. Java Jim naturally grabbed it and ran!"

Pete beamed. "That was fast thinking, Jupe."

"It sure was!" Bob echoed.

"The hand is quicker than the eye," Jupiter said smugly, "especially in the dark! But seriously, fellows, I think Java Jim has told us something he didn't mean to."

"Told us, Jupe?" Bob said. "What did he tell us?"

"That he is after much more than an Oriental sea chest," Jupiter declared. "Did you notice he didn't even ask about that ring, or attempt to take the chest?"

"Wow!" Pete said. "He didn't, did he? He just wanted the book you found!"

"As if he *knew* the book was in the chest," Bob added.

"Or at least suspected it might be," Jupiter said. "I think it was the notebook that Java Jim wanted all along."

"Gee, what kind of notebook could be so important?" Pete wanted to know.

Jupiter held up the notebook papers. "It's a journal, Pete. A kind of diary of day-to-day happenings and actions. I—"

"A journal?" Bob exclaimed. "Gosh, I've just been reading a journal by a survivor of the *Argyll*

Queen wreck." The smallest of the boys related all that had happened at the Historical Society. "There wasn't anything important in the pamphlet manuscript that Professor Shay hadn't told me about, and the journal was just what happened to Angus Gunn for about two years. It told about the wreck, how he got to shore in a boat at dawn when the storm let up, and all about wandering around California until he found a place he liked and built a house."

"Nothing about a treasure?" Pete asked.

Bob shook his head. "And nothing about the Captain, or danger, or anything except building his house. All pretty dull."

But Jupiter didn't think so. "Fellows, I found the thin journal inside a wall of the chest. You see, the chest has a double wall—a thin inner one and a heavy outer wall. Probably to fit the secret compartment in better, or to make the chest watertight. When I examined the chest earlier, I shook it and heard this faint thumping.

"When I looked closely at the inside, I saw that one wall contained a piece of wood that didn't match the rest. The colour was a little off, and the grain was different. A repair had obviously been made, a long time ago. Anyway, I pried off the different board, and poked down in the narrow space between the two walls with a coat hanger, and pulled out the oilskin-wrapped journal!"

"Gee," Pete said, "you think someone hid it there, Jupe?"

"No, I think the inner wall must have been

broken for a while, and the journal slipped down in there accidentally. Then someone fixed the broken side without noticing the journal."

"But Java Jim guessed it was in the chest, and he wants it," Pete said. "But why?"

"Read the front page, Bob," said Jupiter, handing the journal papers to him.

Bob went over to the light at the workbench and read out loud, "*Angus Gunn, Phantom Lake, California, October 29, 1872!* Why, it's the same man who wrote the other journal! The survivor of the *Argyll Queen*!"

"When did the other journal end, Bob?" Jupiter asked.

Bob pulled out his notes. "Let's see. Wait. Yes —the last day of the big journal was October 28, 1872! The new one's the same journal! A continuation no one ever saw!"

"Maybe it tells about the treasure!" Pete exclaimed.

Jupiter shook his head. "I couldn't find anything about treasure in it. It's just like the journal Bob read—what Gunn did, where he went. That's all."

"Then why does Java Jim want it?" Pete wondered. "You think he's just chasing the same old rumours?"

"Maybe it isn't this new journal he wants at all," Bob said.

Jupiter was thinking. "Bob, you said that the Gunn family gave the first journal to the Historical Society *recently*?"

"That's right, Jupe," Bob said. "Hey! That means—"

"That they must still live near here," Jupiter said. "Come on, fellows!"

Jupiter crawled into Tunnel Two, and Bob and Pete followed. The tunnel ended below a trapdoor in the floor of Headquarters. The boys scrambled up and Jupiter got out the telephone book.

"Here it is—Mrs Angus Gunn, 4 Phantom Lake Road! Get our map, Pete."

Jupiter studied the large map while Bob prepared a new cover for the journal papers. Finally the stocky boy announced,

"There! About three miles east in the mountains."

Jupiter grinned. "Tomorrow, fellows, we'll get on our bikes and pay a visit to Mrs Angus Gunn!"

5

Attacked!

THE DAY was clear and cold when the boys cycled out of the salvage yard early the next morning. But by the time they stopped at a side road in the mountains, the sun was hot.

"There it is," Pete said, wiping his brow. "Phantom Lake Road. It goes right on up into the mountains."

"And steep," Jupiter moaned. "We'll have to walk the bikes up. Come on."

The boys pushed their bikes up the side road, winding through tall trees. A creek beside the road, full now in winter, accounted for the trees in the dry mountains.

"I wonder where they got the name?" Bob said. "Phantom Lake, I mean. I never heard of any lakes in our mountains."

Jupiter frowned. "That is odd, Records."

"There are some reservoirs," Pete pointed out.

"Not named Phantom Lake," Bob said, "and I don't—"

All three boys heard the car. Ahead of them and above, coming fast down Phantom Lake Road. They could hear its tyres squealing on the curves long before they could see it. Then the car came into view, careering towards them.

"It's the green VW!" Pete exclaimed.

"Is it Java Jim?" Bob cried.

"Quick!" Jupiter said. "Hide!"

They flung their bikes off the road and jumped into the bushes as the small foreign car bore down on them. It flashed past—and screeched to a skidding stop. A man jumped out and started to run towards them.

"Hey! You kids! Stop right there!"

The man wasn't Java Jim. He was a small, thin, younger man with a thick moustache and wild black hair. He was dressed all in black. He ran towards the boys, his dark eyes blazing.

"What do you kids want—?"

The boys backed away.

"Run!" Pete cried.

They began to run up the edge of the road. The young man shouted again and ran after them. They crashed through the undergrowth.

"Who . . . who is he, Jupe?" Bob said, panting.

Pete said, "Let's get away first, and ask later!"

"Maybe we should stop and talk to—" Jupiter began.

Before he could finish, another sound seemed to fill the woods—the hoofbeats of a galloping horse. The boys paused. A horseman appeared riding hard through the trees to the right of the road. Something long flashed in his hand as he rode.

"Wha . . . what . . ." Pete stammered.

"Look!" Jupiter cried.

The horseman angled past them towards the

green VW. The wild-haired young man had already turned and run back to his car. As the boys watched he got into it, started up, and skidded away in a cloud of dust towards the highway below. The horseman pursued the car for a few yards, then wheeled his horse and galloped back to the boys.

The great horse reared to a stop and the rider glared down at them. He was a short, stocky man with a harsh red face and fiery blue eyes. He wore a tweed jacket and narrow, almost skin-tight plaid trousers. The thing that had flashed in his hand was a long, heavy, basket-hilted sword!

"So! I've got you rascals! You'll make no move now!"

"But—!" Jupiter started to protest.

"Silence!" the horseman thundered. "I'm not knowing what you and that older ruffian are doing here, but I will!"

Pete blurted out hotly, "We weren't with—!"

"You can tell your lies to the police! Now march!"

"But, sir," Jupiter started to say again, "we—"

"March, I said!" the angry horseman commanded.

He waved the long sword menacingly and urged his horse at the boys. They shrank back, and quietly began to march up the road deeper into the mountains.

Ten minutes later the road topped a ridge and dipped down into a high wooded valley surrounded by dry, rocky mountains. At the bottom lay a narrow pond, about twice as long as a football field. There was a small, hilly island in the pond, with pine trees on it, and what looked like some kind of beacon—a tall pole with a lantern on it. A series of stones led from the island across a narrow channel to the shore.

Pete gaped. "Is *that* supposed to be the lake?"

"Ye'll no talk!" the horseman growled behind the boys. "On down with you now."

The boys hurried on down the mountain road in the hot sun. After another moment, Pete whispered,

"Some lake. It's a puddle!"

As the road curved down to the bottom, a house came into view. Set on high ground above the pond, it was a big old three-storied house of roughly plastered stone. A square tower with a battlement formed the middle section of the house and gave it a strange, alien air. Flanking the tower were two wings with dormer windows. The tangled old vines on the walls failed to soften the building's harsh lines.

"Wow!" exclaimed Pete under his breath. "That house looks more like a fortress! You could stand on the tower and spot your enemies miles away!"

"It *is* an odd house," Jupiter whispered back. "In fact, it doesn't seem to belong here at all."

The stocky horseman dismounted. "Inside wi' ye!"

They went into a vast entry hall of panelled wood hung with tapestries, old weapons, and the heads of elk and deer. Faded Oriental rugs lay on the wooden floor. Everything was old and worn. The red-faced man herded them with his sword into a large living-room full of massive old furniture. A fire smouldered in an enormous stone fireplace but the room was still chilly.

A small woman was sitting in a chair in front of the fireplace. A red-headed boy about Bob's size stood beside her. He wore the same tight plaid trousers as the horseman.

"You got him, Rory!" the boy cried.

"That I did not," the horseman said. "The villain escaped in his car, but I've collared his confederates."

"Why," the woman said, "they're only boys, Rory! Surely they can't—?"

"Evil no has to come in full size, Flora Gunn," Rory said. "They're big enough for devils' work." He nodded to the red-headed boy. "You best call the police, Cluny, and we'll get to the bottom of all this breaking in once and for all."

Jupiter came alert. "The man in the Volkswagen broke in here, sir? What did he take?"

The man laughed. "Ay, as if you're not knowing!"

"We don't know!" Pete protested. "We never saw that man! We saw the car, though, because it's been following *us*!"

Jupiter said quietly, "We were coming here to talk to you, Mrs Gunn, when the man passed us on the road. He stopped and chased us. I'm Jupiter Jones from The Jones Salvage Yard in Rocky

Beach, and these are my friends Bob Andrews and Pete Crenshaw. Our bikes are back on the road. They should prove that we didn't come with the man in the Volkswagen."

"Flora!" the horseman said. "It's the police you should—"

"Be quiet, Rory," Mrs Gunn said, and nodded to the boys. "I'm Flora Gunn, boys, this is my son, Cluny, and that is our cousin, Mr Rory McNab. May I ask why you were coming to see me?"

Bob blurted out, "Because of the chest, ma'am!"

"Our salvage yard bought an old Oriental sea chest, ma'am," Jupiter explained. "It has the name *Argyll Queen* in it, and we think it belonged to your ancestor, Angus Gunn. Since we got the chest, some mysterious things have been happening. If you could tell me what the man in the Volkswagen took from your house, it might help explain what's happened."

Mrs Gunn hesitated. "Well, he took nothing, boys. It's the same every time. Someone breaks in, rummages all through what we have left of Great-grandfather Angus's things, and never takes anything at all."

"Nothing?" Pete said, disappointed.

But Jupiter said, "Every time, Mrs Gunn? How many times has your house been broken into recently?"

"Five times in the last six months, I'm afraid."

The red-headed boy, Cluny, burst out, "It's

always old Angus's things they search! I think they're trying to find—"

"The treasure!" Bob exclaimed.

"Mother," Cluny cried eagerly, "they think it's the treasure the burglar is after, too!"

Mrs Gunn smiled. "That old legend of a treasure was proved groundless a long time ago, boys. Cluny has too much imagination."

"Maybe not, Mrs Gunn," Jupiter said, and told them about Java Jim and his interest in the Oriental chest. He showed the ring they had found in the chest.

Mrs Gunn examined the ring. "You found this?"

"Let me see," Rory McNab said, taking the ring. "Bah, it's red glass and brass! Old Angus had a box full of such trinkets for trading. You're fools! People read old Angus's journal and searched for a hundred years and nary a hint of a treasure!"

Mrs Gunn sighed. "Rory is right, boys. Old Angus's journal was the only possible source for a clue to any treasure, and no one ever found such a clue. I'm afraid it was all nonsense."

"Unless," Jupiter said, "everyone read the wrong journal!"

He took the thin second journal from his jacket and held it up in the silent room.

6

A Voice from the Past

"ANOTHER JOURNAL?" Cluny cried.

"What kind o' trick is this?" Rory growled.

Mrs Gunn took the thin journal. She turned some pages slowly, and looked in the front. "It's no trick, Rory. This is old Angus's handwriting, sure enough, and the signature is his." She looked at the boys. "Where did you get it?"

Jupiter told her how he had found the new journal between the walls of the chest. "Whoever repaired the inner wall of the chest didn't notice the journal in the narrow space or know about the secret compartment. If the compartment had ever been opened, the pirate booby trap would have been sprung, and it hadn't been."

Mrs Gunn nodded. "Yes, I remember that old Oriental chest now. I sold it years ago, after my husband passed away. I've had to sell many of old Angus's things to make ends meet. We're not well off, I'm afraid, and this house is expensive to keep up. Without Rory's help and hard work we'd have lost the house long ago."

"Ye'll nae lose the house, Flora," Rory grumbled, "nor need fairy tales o' treasures to keep it."

"The new journal's no fairy tale, Mr McNab," Jupiter said.

"Call me Rory, boy, and I'll admit the journal's real if Flora says so," Rory said grudgingly. "But it no proves the treasure's more than the nonsense of fools."

"But the letter, Rory!" young Cluny cried.

"Letter?" Jupiter repeated.

Rory ignored the leader of the trio. His eyes narrowed. "We'd best have a read o' that journal. Hand it to me."

Cluny took the journal from his mother, and gave it to Rory. The two of them sat on a long bench in front of the smouldering fire and began to read the journal. Mrs Gunn nodded thoughtfully.

"Yes," she said, "if there was a second journal, it would have been in that chest. My husband told me that his grandfather, Angus's son, found the original journal in the chest. Grandfather Gunn always believed there was a treasure, and that the clue to it was in old Angus's journal. But his son —my husband's father—said that the journal told nothing, and the treasure was just a legend."

"Why was Angus's son so sure, Mrs Gunn?" Bob asked.

"Well, there's a letter, you see? Great-grandfather Angus—" She stopped and smiled. "Perhaps I should begin at the beginning, boys. How much do you know about old Angus?"

They told her what they had found out about the wreck of the *Argyll Queen* and the murder of Angus Gunn back in 1872.

"You've read the manuscript the Historical

Society is preparing? Then you know most of the story. I told the Society as much as I could—everything that I'd learned from my husband," Mrs Gunn said. "After the wreck, and his wanderings round California, old Angus found this valley. It reminded him of his old home in the Hi hlands of Scotland—especially because of the pond and its island. In Scotland, Gunn Lodge is on the shores of a long inlet of the sea—Phantom Loch. There's an island in the loch connected to the shore by a series of great boulders, called the Phantom's Steps—very like the little island in our pond."

Jupiter exclaimed, "So old Angus built this house exactly like Gunn Lodge in Scotland! That's why it looks so odd for California."

"That's right, Jupiter," Mrs Gunn acknowledged. "The real Gunn Lodge was originally built in 1352. It was called Gunn Castle then, because it was no more than a fortified tower. You needed a stronghold to protect yourself in those days.

"Over the years," Mrs Gunn went on, "the original tower-house was added on to and remodelled to make the house you see here. The lodge still has details that remind you of a castle, though it couldn't be defended easily any more. The old tower came in handy after the Gunns took to the sea in the seventeenth century. Their wives used to stand on it watching for the ships to return up the loch."

"Same idea as a New England widow's walk," commented Bob.

Pete burst out, "But what about the letter, ma'am?"

"After Angus found the valley and the pond that looked so much like home, he built the house. It took him almost two years. Then he sent for his wife and son. But when they got here from Scotland months later, old Angus was dead and so were his murderers. His wife, Laura, found a letter addressed to her and hidden in an old bed-warmer."

"Something almost no one would use except his wife!" Jupiter said with satisfaction.

"His son thought that, too, when all the rumours of treasure started," Mrs Gunn said. "He was sure the letter was intended to disclose the treasure, and it seemed to refer to old Angus's journal. But Grandfather Gunn never did find a clue in Angus's journal or anywhere else."

"Can we see the letter, ma'am?" Pete urged.

"Of course, boys. It's in my bedroom in a scrapbook."

Jupiter asked, "You don't keep it with old Angus's other things?"

"No, I never did," said Mrs Gunn.

She left the living-room and returned in a moment with a scrapbook. The boys crowded round to read the old, yellowed letter:

Laura, dear
You will be here soon, but lately I fear I am being watched. I must write these last, urgent words in the knowledge that other eyes may see them.

*Remember that I loved you and promised
to give you a golden life. Remember what
I loved at home, and the secret of the loch.
Follow my last course, read what my days
built for you. See the secret in a mirror.*

The boys looked at each other, and read the old letter again.

"According to my husband, Grandfather Gunn was sure that the words *golden life* referred to a treasure left for Laura," Mrs Gunn said. "That last line made him search everything he could see in every mirror in the house. When he found nothing, he decided that the words *read what my days built for you* meant that the clue was in Angus's journal. But he still never found anything."

"Because he didn't have the *second* journal," Jupiter declared. "The letter says *follow my last course.* The word *course* is sailor-talk for a ship's direction, where it's going, its path. The letter is telling Laura to read about what Angus did last for a clue to the treasure—and that has to be in the *second* journal. It covers the last two months before he wrote the letter. What did old Angus do the last two months?"

Rory snorted and threw down the second journal. "He nae did anything about a treasure! All this journal does is tell where he went and what he did to build some surprise for Laura."

"I don't see any clues, fellows," Cluny admitted unhappily.

"I guess I didn't, either," Jupiter confessed. "But . . . Mrs Gunn, what did old Angus love at home, and what is the secret of Phantom Loch?"

"I have no idea what he loved at home, Jupiter," Mrs Gunn said. "The secret of the loch is a very ancient legend back in Scotland. The phantom of an early Gunn is supposed to appear on foggy winter mornings to stand on a crag and stare down the loch, watching for enemies. They say he was killed by Vikings in the ninth century, and is guarding against another raid. The legend of the phantom gave the loch its name."

"A ghost story," Rory snapped. "To add to a treasure fable!"

"The treasure's no fable to Java Jim!" Pete said hotly.

"What about the man in the green VW?" Bob demanded.

"And all the break-ins?" Cluny echoed.

Rory lapsed into a sullen silence.

"Mrs Gunn?" Jupiter said after a moment. "How many people would know what's in the letter and the first journal?"

"Over the years, Jupiter, many people must have read them."

"Then that could explain the break-ins," Jupiter said. "Java Jim must know about them, and must think the letter does refer to a journal. There's a gap of two months between the last entry in the first journal and Angus's murder. Java Jim probably realised there had to be a second journal! So he searched for it!"

"Then he's another big fool," Rory muttered.

"I don't think so," Jupiter said. "Look what Angus said in the letter—*I must write these last, urgent words in the knowledge that other eyes may see them.* So he wrote a puzzle he thought Laura could solve. I'm convinced that Angus *did* hide some treasure, which can be found by solving the puzzle with a clue in the second journal!"

Bob, Pete, and young Cluny nodded eagerly.

"Perhaps so, Jupiter," Mrs Gunn said, "but how could anyone hope to solve the puzzle if Laura couldn't? It was written for her."

"We'll figure it out, ma'am!" Bob cried.

"We've solved lots of puzzles and mysteries!" Pete said.

Jupiter drew himself up taller. "As it happens, Mrs Gunn, solving mysteries and conundrums is our business." He took a card from his pocket and presented it to Mrs Gunn.

Cluny, wide-eyed, read it over his mother's shoulder:

THE THREE INVESTIGATORS

"We Investigate Anything"

? ? ?

First Investigator – JUPITER JONES
Second Investigator – PETER CRENSHAW
Records and Research – BOB ANDREWS

Rory grabbed the card and glared at it. He looked at the boys suspiciously. Jupiter ignored him.

"We would like to offer our services," he said solemnly.

"We sure would!" Pete added.

Cluny urged, "Let them try, Mum! And I'll help!"

"Well." Mrs Gunn smiled. "I see no harm in it, and if there were a treasure we could certainly use it, boys."

"Hurray!" Bob, Pete, and Cluny cried together.

Mrs Gunn laughed. "Then what about some lunch? Treasure hunters need their strength."

Rory threw down the card. "It's some trick, Flora!"

"I don't think so, Rory," Mrs Gunn said.

"Then I wash my hands o' the whole affair," Rory raged, and stamped out of the living-room.

Jupiter watched him go, and frowned.

7

Ghost Town!

As soon as lunch was over, Rory McNab left, muttering that he was going to cut some Christmas greens from pines along the road. The boys and Mrs Gunn returned to the living-room and began to study the second journal carefully.

"First, fellows," Jupiter said, "you'll notice that the journal isn't a true diary. Angus didn't write about his thoughts or plans, nor did he really describe anything. Most entries are brief, a line or two—*Worked in the yard today* and *Saw an eagle.* More like a ship's log—just the facts and no explanations."

"The other journal's just like that, too," Bob said.

"So most entries don't tell us anything," Jupiter went on. "But Angus says in the letter to follow his course and read what his days built. He didn't want Laura to note all he did, but only where he *went* and what he *built*."

Cluny looked at the journal. "Well, the first entry's about going somewhere—*Today began work on Laura's surprise. First to Powder Gulch for men and sluice timber.*"

"He *was* building something!" Pete exclaimed.

"As the letter says," Jupiter agreed. "What next, Cluny?"

The red-headed boy turned several pages. "Nothing for two weeks. Just little notes—*Saw hawk*, and that sort of thing. Then he went to an island."

"Mrs Gunn?" Jupiter said. "What was Laura's surprise?"

"I have no idea," Mrs Gunn said. "Perhaps furniture?"

"Well, we'll think about that later," Jupiter decided. "Men and sluice timber. A sluice is a trough to carry water. Miners used to wash gold out of ore with a sluice. Is there a mine here at Phantom Lake, Cluny?"

"Not that I ever heard," Cluny said. "You mean a gold mine?"

"Maybe Angus built a secret mine!" Pete exclaimed.

"That's possible, Second," Jupiter conceded. "But I've got a hunch we won't find our answers here. Angus said to *follow* his course, as if the clue is somewhere he *went*. Fellows, we'll go to Powder Gulch!"

"Is Powder Gulch around here?" asked Pete.

Cluny said, "It's only a mile or so up the highway."

"I'm surprised you don't know about it, Pete," Jupiter said. "It's quite famous in local history. I've read all about it. It—"

Bob jumped up. "The old ghost town! Sure!"

54

"A . . . a ghost town?" Pete gulped. "Do we have to go?"

"We do," Jupiter declared, and stood up. "And we'll go right now!"

The battered sign that read "Powder Gulch" pointed off the highway and along a narrow dirt road. The four boys cycled down the road and ten minutes later saw the ghost town below.

They stopped to study the town. Ruined old shacks were scattered along a dry creek bed, and dilapidated buildings with high false fronts lined the single street. One large building was labelled "Saloon". Another had "General Store" clearly painted on it. A squat adobe building was marked "Jail". There were also a blacksmith shop and livery stable. At the far end of the street, in the side of a mountain, stood the dark entrance to the gold mine that was the reason for the town in the old days.

"This town was abandoned about 1890 when the mine ran out," Jupiter explained. "The creek was then dammed to make a reservoir."

Pete groaned. "What can we expect to find here after a hundred years, Jupe?"

"I don't know, Second," Jupiter admitted. "But I'm certain Angus Gunn wanted Laura to look here. Maybe there was a newspaper once. Perhaps we can find some old issues around."

"Maybe there's even an old morgue," said Bob, referring to the clipping files that newspapers maintain.

"I hope we don't end up in a different kind of morgue!" Pete said flatly.

"Come on," Jupiter said.

They cycled on down to the edge of the old ghost town—and stopped! A locked gate faced them. The entire ghost town was circled by a high fence!

"It's all fenced in!" Cluny cried. "And those signs painted on the buildings look new! You think someone's living here again?"

"I . . . don't know," Jupiter said.

The boys waited a minute, straining to hear any signs of life in the town. But Powder Gulch remained ominously silent.

"I guess we'll have to climb the fence, fellows," Jupe said at last.

Dropping their bikes, the boys quietly started to climb. Moments later they stood on the other side looking up the dusty street.

"Pete, you and Bob look through the buildings on the left side of the street," Jupiter decided nervously. "Cluny and I will take the jail and livery stable on the right, and go on to the mine. See if you can find anything about Angus Gunn and sluice timber."

Bob and Pete nodded, and went first to the general store. They tiptoed inside and stopped, amazed. The store looked exactly as it must have a hundred years ago! The shelves were full of goods. Barrels of dried apples and flour, hardware, and leather harness crowded the low, dim room. Old-fashioned guns that shone like new hung on the walls. The long counter was clean and polished!

"Maybe someone *is* living here again!" Bob exclaimed softly.

"B-but . . . not someone from today," Pete stammered. "Everything here looks like a hundred years ago. A store for . . . for ghosts!"

Bob gulped and nodded. "This is just the way the store must have been way back. As if . . . as if no one ever left! Even . . . Pete! On the counter! There's an old ledger!"

Warily, the two boys went over to the counter. The old ledger lay open, showing names written next to orders for goods. Bob's hands shook as he turned the pages to the entries for October 29, 1872. Pete read over his shoulder,

"*Angus Gunn, Phantom Lake—200 board-ft. sluice timber with supports; 2 barrels flour; 1 barrel beef; 4 cases dried beans.*" Pete blinked. "Wow, he bought food for an army!"

"He had to feed the men he hired here," Bob guessed. "There must have been a lot of them. Do you see anything else, Pete?"

Pete shook his head. "Not in here."

They hurried out of the eerie general store. The saloon was next.

"Saloons were community centres back then," Bob said. "A place to meet people and leave messages. Angus probably stopped for a drink here."

The saloon was one large, dark room with a door at the rear that led to sleeping rooms. An ornate upright piano stood on the left, clean and shiny. Rows of bottles stood full behind the long, polished bar. At the rear a round table was covered with bottles and half-full glasses and scattered cards, as if a poker game were in progress.

"It . . . it's just like the store," Pete said uneasily. "As if the miners are still here and just went out for a minute, and—"

Pete got no further. The loud noise of many voices suddenly filled the old saloon! The piano began to play a lively tune from the wild frontier past—but no one was at it! Glasses and bottles clinked. The sounds of drinking and shouting shook the room. There was a crash at the poker table in the rear—and a shadowy shape seemed to rise from it.

"Freeze, strangers!" a hollow voice said menacingly.

The dark, shadowy figure had a pistol in each ghostly hand!

"A ghost!" Pete cried. "Run, Bob!"

Stumbling over each other, they ran pell-mell from the old saloon. The invisible crowd roared behind them, and the piano still played. Out on the hot street they ran madly towards the mine.

Inside the mine, the long tunnel was lighted! They ran on down the sloping shaft, and saw Jupiter and Cluny ahead.

"Jupe! A ghost attacked—!" Pete began, and stopped.

Jupiter and Cluny were pale and shaking and staring ahead down the dim mine shaft. Bob and

Pete became aware of noises—the sound of water dripping, of machinery clanking, and then wild, almost insane laughter. A shot exploded in the mine, seemed to zing past the boys, and reverberated on up the tunnel.

"Wha-what . . . is it, Jupe?" Bob stammered.

Jupiter swallowed hard. "I . . . I don't know. We came in here, and . . . and . . . he shot at us! He—"

Pete and Bob saw him!

Not more than twenty feet ahead in the dim tunnel, he stood aiming an old rifle at them—a grizzled, bearded miner in a red wool shirt and buckskin trousers and high leather boots!

"We know how to deal with claim-jumpers!" the apparition said in an echoing voice.

Laughing nastily, the dim shape raised the rifle and pulled the trigger!

8

A Ghost to the Rescue

THE SHOT exploded straight at the boys! And another shot! At point-blank range!

Ashen-faced, Pete stood in the shaft with his eyes shut.

"Am . . . am I . . . hit?" he wailed.

The tall investigator opened his eyes and looked at the others. They were all pale.

"He missed us!" Bob cried.

Cluny stammered, "He . . . he's just scaring us, fellows!"

"But what does he—?" Pete began.

The bearded apparition laughed wildly again, raised the old rifle once more, and called out nastily, "We know how to deal with claim-jumpers!"

And pulled the trigger again!

Two shots exploded once more at point-blank range.

"Missed us again!" Cluny cried. The red-headed boy glared at the old miner and took a step forward. "What do you want from—?"

"Wait, Cluny!" Jupiter said suddenly, staring at the crazy old miner. "Everyone watch!"

They watched the old miner warily. The noises

of water and machinery still sounded through the mine. After a long minute, there was a faint click and whir, and the old miner laughed his wild laugh. His rifle rose!

"We know how to deal with claim-jumpers!" he boomed, pulling the trigger. Two more shots rang out—and missed!

"It's a fake!" Jupiter cried, and began to laugh. "It's a mechanical dummy, men! With a recording in it. The noises are just some kind of sound track."

Bob suddenly groaned. "Am I dumb! I remember now! I read about it in the newspaper, fellows. They're restoring Powder Gulch and making it into a tourist attraction! Rides, and ghosts, and western shows. That's why the town's locked up."

"Of course," Jupiter said glumly. "I read that, too. Some time ago."

Pete walked up to the old miner and touched the face. "It's moulded plastic. Boy, it sure looks real. I guess our ghost in the saloon was a fake, too. They sure do some job on dummies these days."

"They do," Jupiter agreed, "but we have other matters to think about. Has anyone seen anything that could be a clue to Angus Gunn's plans?"

Bob told him about the ledger in the general store, and the food old Angus had bought for a lot of men.

"Or if not many men, a long job of building something," Jupiter reasoned. "So we know that whatever Angus built for a surprise for Laura was a pretty big job. What we don't know yet is what it was, or where he built it." He opened the thin journal and frowned at it. "There just isn't enough in the entry for October 29 to help."

"We never did look for messages in the saloon," Pete said.

"All right, we'll go back there next," Jupiter said, closing the journal. "Then we'll try the jail —the sheriff back then might have left some records—and look for a newspaper office."

They started back out of the old mine. Pete and Bob noticed details they'd missed on the way in —refurbished mining carts, some old tools, and another dummy—a black-bearded miner with a pick in his hands.

Pete grinned. "Boy, those plastic dummies are real-looking. That one with the pick looks like—"

The black-bearded miner dropped the pickaxe, jumped at Jupiter, grabbed the journal, and ran out of the mine shaft!

"Java Jim!" Bob gasped.

The boys stood paralysed by the shock of the dummy leaping to life. Then Jupiter recovered.

"He got the journal! After him!"

They pounded along the dimly lit mine shaft and out into the hot afternoon sun.

"There he goes!" Cluny cried.

The short sailor was far down the main street, running hard.

"Stop, you thief!" Pete yelled.

"He's getting away!" Cluny shouted. "Stop, robber!"

Java Jim glanced back with a laugh and ran

past the saloon—just as a shadowy figure in black appeared in the doorway. A figure with a big, black pistol in each hand!

"It's our ghost!" Pete gulped.

Java Jim saw the menacing, wraithlike figure in the saloon doorway. With a cry, the bearded sailor veered away from the saloon—and fell sprawling over an old horse trough. The journal flew from his hand. He scrambled up, then stumbled again.

"He's a thief!" Pete yelled. "Grab him!"

The "ghost" looked towards the boys, and then started down the steps of the wooden sidewalk towards Java Jim. His pistols caught the sunlight. Java Jim didn't wait. He turned and ran off behind the buildings to the fence, scrambled over, and vanished into the thick, dry undergrowth along the creek bed.

The boys ran up to the "ghost." Outside in the light, he was just a man dressed in black western clothes. Jupiter picked up the thin journal where Java Jim had dropped it.

"You boys shouldn't be in here," the "ghost" said. "You better tell me what this is all about, and give me that book if it belongs to this town."

"It doesn't, sir," Jupiter said. "We're sorry we climbed the fence, but we didn't know anyone was here, and we had to investigate." He explained that they were trying to discover Angus Gunn's business in Powder Gulch. "You certainly scared us with your tricks!"

The "ghost" grinned. "I decided to practise our

special effects on you. I'm the caretaker here."
He rubbed his jaw. "Angus Gunn, eh? Maybe I
can help. I've got all the old records in my office.
If your Angus Gunn did anything here, I'll find
it."

They went through the saloon into a small
office. The caretaker opened a filing cabinet. "All
the names in the old records have been indexed
and cross-referenced, boys. Part of the work of the
restoration. Let's see what we have for Gunn."

He read a file and shook his head. "Just two
references. The purchase you saw in the general
store, and a two-line notice in the Gulch newspaper for 1872 offering a short job for miners.
That's all."

"A dead end," Pete groaned. "We—"

They heard a voice yelling outside. "Boys! . . .
Cluny Gunn! . . . You boys . . . !"

"It's Rory!" Cluny said.

They hurried through the saloon. Rory McNab
stood out in the street with the man Bob had
talked to at the Historical Society—Professor
Shay. The round-faced little professor hurried up
to the boys.

"Boys! You gave us quite a turn! I bumped
into Mr McNab outside the gates. He told me you
were supposed to be here, and then we found your
bikes. We were afraid something had happened
to—"

"Trespassing!" Rory snapped. "I knew ye'd get
into trouble. That's why I came after—to see ye
didna' hurt yersels!"

"No harm done, Mr McNab," the caretaker said. "Maybe Professor Shay would be interested in the boys' comments on our special effects. The professor is our historical adviser, boys. The Society is helping with the restoration."

"Yes, yes, but later!" Professor Shay said, his eyes bright behind his rimless glasses. He waved goodbye to the caretaker and steered the boys down the street. "What is this about a second Angus Gunn journal, boys? You found one? You think there could be a treasure? What a discovery. Historical! Tell me, quickly!"

Jupiter told about the second journal and Java Jim's interest in it. Professor Shay's round face turned purple.

"What?" he cried. "This . . . this person! Java Jim? He's trying to steal the Gunns' treasure? To use it for his own gain, sell it in bits, perhaps melt the gold? Monstrous! Why, it would be historically priceless! An East Indian pirate hoard intact! Our Society's museum would be famous. But you found no clue here?"

"Well," Jupiter said slowly, "we have learned that whatever Angus built for his wife was a big job."

"Yes, I see, but not here," Professor Shay said. "At Phantom Lake! I'm an expert on this area. Perhaps I can see what you boys can't. Put your bikes in my car, and we'll drive to Phantom Lake. It would be a crime to lose the treasure to that Java Jim!"

C

Rory sneered at Professor Shay, "Another fool you are!"

"What? And what do you know, McNab?" the professor said. "I think the boys may be right! Get your bikes, boys."

The gates were open now. The boys put their bikes into the back of Professor Shay's station wagon. Rory went off to his own car. Jupiter gave him a puzzled look.

9

The Mysterious Light

By LATE afternoon, Professor Shay had led the boys over every foot of the small valley and up half the hills. They had looked down on Phantom Lake and its small island from every angle. The boys had trotted round the house after the excited little professor three times. And they found exactly nothing!

They gathered on the terrace of the big house in the late sun. Mrs Gunn watched the boys and the professor with sympathy. Rory smoked his pipe with a sardonic smile.

"Nothing," Professor Shay said in dejection. "Angus Gunn built nothing big except the house, and it's been searched for years. And there's no trace of that sluice timber."

Rory laughed. "You're all daft! If old Angus did build something of sluice timber, it'd be long gone now. And if any treasure ever existed, which it nae did, ye'll no' find it now."

"We will!" Bob cried.

"Of course you will, boys," Mrs Gunn said, looking severely at Rory. "Perhaps the treasure won't be a *real* treasure, but I'm sure you'll find something."

"Gee, Mum," Cluny said, "you sound like you don't believe there's a treasure, either!"

Jupiter was rereading the letter of Angus Gunn. "If we just knew a little more. I'm convinced there's a key, but it was all so long ago. What *did* old Angus love at home?"

Mrs Gunn shook her head. "While you boys were at Powder Gulch, I took the time to reread most of Laura's letters. She writes a lot of Angus's love of the Gunn land in Scotland, of the magnificent view down the narrow loch, but that's all. Nothing at all specific, Jupiter."

"It does seem almost hopeless," Professor Shay said.

"I admit it seems a most difficult problem," Jupiter agreed with a long sigh.

Cluny cried, "You're not going to give up, Jupiter?"

"Hunh!" Pete said. "You sure don't know Jupe! He's only getting started!"

"I wouldn't blame you boys for giving up," Mrs Gunn said.

"I don't think it's time to give up yet," said Jupiter. "Old Angus didn't say *where* we'd find a clue, and we've taken only the first step. It's time for the second step."

He opened the thin journal. "The next entry that appears significant is for November 11, 1872. *This day sailed to the island of the cypresses. Very nearly foundered in sou'wester and high sea due to load in boat. Squire of the island agreed to my proposal, and I returned home by noon well satisfied. Work on*

68

Laura's present goes forward well. The next week or so is just his daily round at home."

"Jupe! He says his boat was *loaded*," Pete pointed out.

"Yes," Jupiter nodded. "The island may be the answer."

"But," Cluny asked, "where is it? I've never heard of any island of cypresses round here."

"Neither have I," Jupiter admitted. "Pete?"

Pete, who was the yachtsman of the trio and knew the local waters well, took the journal. "I don't think that's its name. It might not have had a name then. All the big Channel Islands did, so this one is probably a small island just off the coast. It has to be near, because Angus got there and back in half a day. It sounds like it was owned by one family, and it must have had cypresses. I'll look it up."

"I'll go, too," Professor Shay exclaimed. "I own a sailing-boat, and we can take it—if the island isn't too far from Rocky Beach."

Rory stood up. "Phantoms, ghosts, islands without names, a man dead a hundred years! Ye've all gone crazy!"

The Scotsman stomped off the terrace as Mrs Gunn shook her head and smiled.

"Don't mind Rory too much," she said. "He has a terrible temper and no use for impractical things, but he's really a good man. We've had a difficult time since Cluny's father passed away, and Rory made the last year much easier. I think he's tired out from his trip."

"Trip?" Jupiter asked sharply. "Rory's been away, ma'am?"

"To Santa Barbara, yes. He went for three days to sell our avocados. He only returned last night."

Jupiter's face clouded. "Just who is Rory, ma'am? He's only been here a year?"

"He's a distant cousin of my husband's from Scotland. He came for a visit, and stayed to help. He's a proud man, and stubborn, and won't take any pay. Just his room and board as part of the family."

Jupiter stood up on the terrace and nodded to Bob and Pete.

"We better get home now, ma'am. It's late," he said.

"I'll drive you," Professor Shay said.

Their bikes were already in Professor Shay's station wagon. Soon they were driving down the side road and out on to the highway to Rocky Beach.

"Professor Shay," Jupiter said suddenly, "one thing puzzles me. How do you think Java Jim knows so much about the Gunns and the letter?"

"I'm not sure, Jupiter," the professor replied. "The rumours of the treasure are well known locally, of course. Still, your Java Jim doesn't appear to be a local. Perhaps he's some descendant of another *Argyll Queen* survivor! Even the Captain."

"Gosh," Bob said. "That could explain it, Jupe."

"I suppose so," Jupiter said slowly.

Professor Shay dropped the boys at the salvage yard half an hour before dinnertime. They scrambled through Tunnel Two into Headquarters.

"Jupe, I've been thinking," Pete said. "How can we be sure old Angus didn't build a mine at Phantom Lake—a hidden mine? Secret!"

"We can't, Second," Jupiter said. "But we'd need some definite clue to find it then. And what would the legend of the phantom in Scotland have to do with a mine? Or a mirror?"

Bob said, "Mrs Gunn told us that the phantom was supposed to watch for Vikings on the lake in Scotland. Maybe old Angus meant that! The phantom stares at the lake—the treasure's somewhere *in* that pond!"

"That's possible, too, Records," Jupiter agreed. "But we'd still need a clue to know just where." Jupiter paused. "Did you two hear what Mrs Gunn told us about Rory, men?"

"Sure," Pete said. "He's a big help and a hard worker."

"And he's got a bad temper," Bob said. "Some news!"

"And," Jupiter said, "he was away from Phantom Lake for three days until last night! Which means, fellows, that he could have been in Rocky Beach yesterday when Java Jim attacked us, and at the roadside museum, and in San Francisco the day before!"

"You mean he could be working with Java Jim to steal the treasure," Bob said. "He'd sure know all about the letter and Phantom Lake and maybe the things Mrs Gunn sold."

"Yes, he would," Jupiter said grimly. "Pete, I want you to identify the island of cypresses tonight. We'll all meet tomorrow morning at Professor Shay's boat!"

After dinner, Jupiter helped Uncle Titus and Aunt Mathilda decorate the Christmas tree. At ten o'clock the telephone rang.

It was Pete. "It's Cabrillo Island, Jupe. The old Cabrillo family owned it in 1872. It's got cypresses all over it. It's only a mile offshore, about two miles north of our harbour."

"Good work, Second!" Jupiter said.

He hung up and went upstairs to his room. Before switching on the light, he walked over to the front window to look at the Christmas lights of Rocky Beach. Many of the houses on the other side of the salvage yard were colourfully lit.

He was about to turn away when a faint flash of light caught his eye. He stared in its direction, and saw another flash, and another. Jupiter looked puzzled. There were no houses where the flash came from. As the flashes of light continued, he suddenly realised their source—the salvage yard, just where Headquarters was hidden!

The flashes were coming from inside Headquarters—through the skylight in the trailer's roof!

Quickly Jupiter slipped downstairs and across the street to the salvage yard. The front gate was properly locked. He turned and ran to the corner where his workshop was. Here was another secret entrance to the yard—two loose boards in a section of green-painted fence.

Cautiously Jupe climbed through Green Gate One into his workshop. He saw that the flashes of light had stopped. No one was near Tunnel Two. He crept round some piles of junk to check Easy Three.

The old wooden door of Easy Three was broken open, and beyond it the trailer door stood ajar!

Inside the trailer Jupiter saw Angus Gunn's journal on the desk where he had left it. It was open to the last entry. He knew then what had caused the flashes—someone had broken into Headquarters and photographed the journal!

Jupiter wedged the Easy Three door back into place and walked slowly home. Now someone else knew Angus Gunn's last course!

10

The Phantom

A MIST HUNG over Rocky Beach harbour the next morning as Pete, Bob, and Jupiter cycled up to the marina. Cluny was already waiting with his bike at Professor Shay's boat. The red-headed boy was shivering in the clammy cold, but he grinned when he saw The Three Investigators.

"I've been thinking all night, fellows," Cluny said, "and I'm sure the 'load' in old Angus's boat was the treasure! I know we'll find it today!"

"I do feel optimistic, Cluny," Jupiter agreed. "It would—"

Professor Shay's station wagon drove up and screeched to a stop. The pink-faced little professor jumped out and ran up to the boys.

"Sorry I'm late, boys, but there was trouble at the Historical Society this morning. Someone broke in and tried to steal the *Argyll Queen* file! A man with a black beard!"

"Java Jim!" Pete and Bob cried together.

Professor Shay nodded. "Sounds like him to me."

"But why?" Cluny wondered. "Everyone knows all about the *Argyll Queen*'s story."

"Unless   everyone   overlooked   something,"

THE SECRET OF PHANTOM LAKE

Jupiter said. He told them about the intruder who had photographed the second journal the night before.

"Then Java Jim has the journal now!" Professor Shay cried. "He may be ahead of us, on the island already!" He looked out at the sea through the mist. "But can we sail in this weather, boys?"

Pete nodded. "Visibility's over a mile offshore —the fog doesn't thicken until farther out. It's like that most of the time round here. And your boat's big and sturdy."

"Then let's hurry, boys!" Professor Shay said.

They piled on to the broad, 25-foot sailing-boat, and Professor Shay started the auxiliary engine. Soon they had left the harbour. Pete took the helm and set a course north. Professor Shay and the three other boys huddled in the cabin. Even their heavy sweaters weren't enough protection against the December morning chill.

"Cabrillo Island didn't have a name until 1890. Then it was named after its owners," Pete explained. "It's a really small island, abandoned now. There's a good cove on the near side."

There was little wind, so Pete continued to use auxiliary. The others remained below until Pete said,

"There it is, fellows!"

The small, high island loomed up a mile ahead in the mist. As they came closer, they could see the cypresses on it, and a tall chimney that jutted up behind one of the island's two hills. It was a bleak and rocky place, ghostly in the mist. A solid bank of fog lay beyond it, out at sea.

Pete steered into a sheltered cove on the mainland side, and they tied up to a rotting old pier. They all scrambled out and stood on the shore looking at the barren, rocky land. Here and there grew stunted old cypresses with sparse foliage. The trees had been twisted into grotesque shapes by the winds.

"Gosh," Bob said in sudden dismay, "if old Angus did bury the treasure here, how do we find it after a hundred years? It could be anywhere!"

"No, Records, I considered that all last night," Jupiter said. "I'm convinced that Angus wouldn't have *buried* the treasure. First, he knew that the Captain of the *Argyll Queen* was after him, and newly dug dirt is easy for anyone to see. Second, he wanted Laura to find it, and even a few months could obliterate all traces of something buried.

"No," the stout leader of the trio went on, "I think he would have *hidden* it somewhere, but marked it with a clear sign that Laura would recognise. A sign that would last a long time, because he couldn't be sure how long Laura might take to find it!"

Cluny had an idea. "Could Angus have built something here for Laura? Maybe bought some land on the island as a surprise?"

"Yes, I've thought of that," Jupiter said. "We'll look for something built of timber, or something identified with the Gunns."

"The letter says to follow his course and read what his days built," Bob said. "That's the general direction. Then it talks about the phantom and a mirror. Those could be the signs!"

"Exactly!" Jupiter said. "But the journal says Angus made some proposal to the squire of this island—maybe for permission to hide something here! So we'll look at the house with the chimney up there first. There could be records in the house."

They climbed up the saddle between the two small hills, and reached a sheltered hollow near the top. The chimney stood tall in the hollow— but nothing else! The chimney, a massive stone fireplace, and a stone hearth, surrounded by bare, rocky ground.

"The house is gone," Pete moaned. "There goes our chance of finding a mirror or records, Jupe."

"Look!" Bob pointed.

Fresh dirt outlined a big, flat slab in the centre of the stone hearth. The slab had evidently been pried up, then dropped back into place.

"Someone's been here ahead of us," Professor Shay cried. "Not long ago from the look of that dirt!"

They looked uneasily round at the bleak hills and twisted cypresses. Nothing moved but streamers of mist.

"Let's see what's under that slab," Bob said.

He and Pete moved the heavy stone slab away. Everyone looked down into an empty hole.

"Nothing in the hole," Pete declared, "and I don't think there ever was—at least recently.

The dirt's dry and loose, with no marks in it, fellows."

"But someone thought there might be," Jupiter said. "See, he scraped dirt from the hearth until he found the slab."

"There wasn't another boat in the cove," Pete said, "but there's a small beach round a point just beyond the cove."

"We'll spread out and find him!" Professor Shay decided. "But be careful. I'll be in the centre. If you see anyone, yell, and run to me."

"Look for anything that might be a sign, too," Jupiter added. "Maybe a cave, a pile of rocks, or something carved in rock."

Everyone nodded nervously. Facing north, they spread out in a line towards each side of the tiny island. As they moved forward through the thickening mist, they began to lose sight of each other. Cluny, on the far left, could see only Pete through the mist.

Cluny was moving up the steepest edge of the westernmost hill. The sea and thicker fog lay to his left. A tendril of thick fog drifted round him until he couldn't even see Pete. Nervous, looking hard for the stranger and listening for any sound, Cluny missed his footing and fell. He slid down the slope in a hail of loose stones.

"Oooof!" he grunted, and scrambled up—and saw it!

Through the drifting fog, a ghostly figure stared down at Cluny from an incline! A twisted black shape with a hump on its back and an evil, pointed face with a hooked nose and one enormous eye!

"It's the phantom!" Cluny screamed. "Help!"

The phantom moved towards Cluny, reaching its long, misshapen arms out to grab him!

11

The Intruder

"Help! Help!" Cluny shouted, cringing from the menacing phantom.

Pete came pounding up through the fog. "What is it!"

"The phantom!" Cluny pointed. "There!"

Pete gulped and shrank back from the grotesque figure. The phantom's single eye moved, followed him.

Then Professor Shay arrived, and Jupiter and Bob came panting up. As they stared at the ghostly shape, the fog suddenly thinned. Bob cried:

"It's a tree!"

"One of the cypresses, twisted by the wind!" Professor Shay added.

The hunchbacked phantom was only a twisted, stunted tree trunk with branches bent out like arms. The "head" was a gnarled stump at the top with a hole in it. Fog drifting behind the hole gave the effect of a moving eye.

"Phew!" Cluny said with relief. "It sure looked like the phantom!"

Suddenly Jupiter exclaimed, "Fellows! It *is* the

phantom! Don't you see? It must be old Angus's sign!"

"The sign?" Pete asked.

"You really think so, Jupe?" Bob cried.

Professor Shay narrowed his eyes behind his rimless glasses. "By Caesar, I think Jupiter must be right! Search round the tree, boys, for a hiding place! The treasure could be here!"

"I'll look on the left!" Cluny said.

"I'll take the right!" Bob joined in.

Professor Shay said, "You climb up above, Jupiter. I'll look round the base of the rise!"

Pete was left standing alone as the others swarmed round the grotesque little tree. He looked to the right, and then to the left. He looked behind him, and then up the rise.

"Fellows," Pete said slowly.

They didn't hear him, or ignored him. They were poking at the thin dirt round the tree and turning over every rock they could find. Professor Shay was probing a crevice with a long stick.

"Fellows," Pete said again, "I don't think you're going to find anything."

Jupiter stopped scraping the dirt. "What? Why, Second?"

Pete shook his head. "I don't think old Angus would have used that tree for his phantom sign, guys."

"What are you talking about, Peter?" Professor Shay snapped. "Why don't you help us—"

"Look over there." Pete pointed to the right.

"Up on the slope—it looks to me like two more phantoms!"

Two ghostly shapes loomed in the mist.

"And there." Pete motioned behind him. "Three more phantoms!"

As the rising wind blew away the thicker mist, more and more of the twisted trees appeared. Everyone stopped digging and looked at them. Professor Shay groaned and threw his stick away.

"They're all cypresses! Seen from the right angle, almost every one of them would look like some kind of phantom!"

Jupiter nodded sadly. "Pete's right. There are too many phantom trees for old Angus to have picked *one* as a sign. Or else—"

"Or else what, Jupe?" Pete asked.

"Or else Angus made a mistake and did pick one to mark the treasure," Jupiter said. "It would take months and months to dig round all the cypresses! We might never find it!"

"I'm afraid," Professor Shay said, "we're beaten, boys."

"Only if old Angus did hide the treasure on the island," Jupiter said. "But—"

The stocky boy was interrupted by a sudden shower of pebbles and rocks that rolled down the slope. He looked up. The mist was almost gone now, and he could see another phantom shape standing on the crest of the hill.

"Just another cypress!" Cluny laughed.

"But," Jupiter said, "a tree can't make stones roll unless—"

"Unless it can move!" Pete said.

"It *is* moving!" Professor Shay cried. "That's no phantom tree, that's a man up there! You! Stop!"

The figure on the crest vanished. A sound of running carried from the other side of the hill.

"Quick, boys!" Professor Shay shouted. "Stop him!"

He ran up the slope with the boys behind him. From the top he could see a distant figure running hard, headed off to the right as if to circle round to the cove.

"He must have a boat," the professor said, panting. "Cut him off!"

They turned and raced back down the hill towards the cove. Pete and Cluny soon outstripped the others and reached the cove in minutes. But the fleeing man was nowhere in sight!

"Over there!" Jupe shouted from the higher ground behind them. "To your left!"

The running figure was just disappearing over a ridge to the north of the cove. Pete and Cluny ran in pursuit. Bob and Professor Shay turned off towards the ridge. Jupiter slowly puffed along far behind them.

Bob and Professor Shay reached the ridge first, with Pete and Cluny close behind. A small, narrow beach lay before them at the foot of the ridge. The fleeing man was already in his motorboat. As he headed the boat away from the island, he looked back for a moment, and the pursuers saw his face.

"It's the man in the green VW!" Bob cried.

Professor Shay stared out at the thin young man with the black moustache and wild black hair.

"Why," the professor said, "it's young Stebbins! Stop, you young villain!"

The motorboat moved farther away from the island.

"The young rascal!" Professor Shay roared. "Quick, to my boat!"

They ran again to the cove. On the way they met Jupiter, still puffing towards the little beach! The portly leader of the Investigators looked at them hopelessly as they raced past him going the opposite way.

"Oh, no!" he groaned, and turned to pant after them again.

The lines were untied, the engine was started, and Pete was ready at the helm when Jupiter finally arrived and collapsed in the boat. Pete steered for the open water. The motorboat was only a few hundred yards ahead.

"Full speed, Peter! Catch him!" Professor Shay urged, and shook his fist towards the motorboat. "Stebbins, you thief!"

Still panting, Jupiter sat up. "You know him, Professor? The young man in the VW? Who is he?"

"My former assistant, young Stebbins," Professor Shay raged. "He was a graduate student over at Ruxton University, a poor young man, and I tried to help him. But he stole from me! He tried to sell valuable historical items from the Society's museum. I had to fire him, and he was sent to prison for a year!"

The motorboat was much farther ahead now, almost a half a mile.

"We'll never catch him," Pete said. "We're too slow."

Professor Shay glared towards the now distant motorboat.

"You wondered how Java Jim knew so much about the treasure and the Gunns, Jupiter," he said. "There's your answer! I recall now that Stebbins was very interested in the *Argyll Queen* and old Angus Gunn! He must have escaped, or been paroled. Now he's up to his old tricks. He's probably working with your Java Jim, by Caesar! He's a most dangerous young criminal!"

"Stebbins must have been the one who photographed the journal at Headquarters last night," Bob decided.

"Yes," Jupiter agreed. "That's how he knew about the island. But he didn't find anything. If he had, he wouldn't have stood around there watching us."

"That makes us even," Bob said. "We didn't find anything, either."

Bob's words cast a pall over the sailing-boat, and they sailed the rest of the way in silence. Professor Shay stared after the now vanished motorboat. When they docked in the marina, there was no sign of Stebbins, his boat, or his Volkswagen.

"I shall report that villain to the police at once,"

Professor Shay said angrily. "He did break into your office last night."

"I didn't actually see him, sir," Jupiter pointed out.

"But you know he did, and at least I can alert the police to the young blackguard!"

"What a day!" said Pete. "We let a crook slip out of our hands, and we couldn't find the treasure."

The professor shook his head slowly. "I'm sorry, boys. This treasure hunt looks hopeless. Perhaps a hundred years is just too long ago."

"I must admit we're making little progress," Jupiter said.

Cluny cried, "There's still more than a month left in the second journal, fellows! Don't stop now!"

"I'm afraid," Professor Shay said sadly, "if you do go on, I'll have to leave it to you boys. I mustn't neglect my work. But I'll be most eager to hear if you do discover something."

They watched the professor walk to his station wagon and drive off. Cluny looked at the boys hopefully.

"Jupe?" Pete said. "We're not quitting, are we?"

"We'd better all go to lunch," Jupiter said unhappily. "I want to think awhile. Then we'll go to Phantom Lake and decide." He sighed. "Something in this case is eluding me."

Dejected, the boys got on their bikes and started home.

12

A New Danger

BOB HAD JUST finished his lunch when his mother called to him that Jupiter was on the telephone.

"I believe we made a completely erroneous assumption, Records!" Jupiter announced eagerly. "It gives me an entirely new conception of old Angus's puzzle!"

Bob grinned as he held the receiver. For once he wasn't bothered by Jupiter's big words. It was the old Jupe talking again, all traces of dejection gone.

"Meet at the yard," Jupiter instructed. "I have a plan!"

Bob hung up and got his bike. When he arrived at the salvage yard, he saw Jupiter and Pete standing by the pickup truck with Hans. He loaded his bike into the truck at Jupe's direction, then climbed in with the others. Hans drove off.

"I told Uncle Titus that Mrs Gunn might have some junk to sell, which is true," Jupiter explained, but said nothing more. Pete and Bob knew better than to question him. The stocky boy never revealed his surprises and deductions until he was ready.

Cluny was standing on the steps of Gunn Lodge when the truck drove up. Jupiter asked for Cluny's mother. The red-headed boy led them round the house to an old stone-and-wood shed at the back. Inside, Mrs Gunn was repotting a large hibiscus in a big redwood tub.

"Ma'am," Jupiter said at once, "we all assumed that the load Angus had in his boat on the trip to the island was something he *took* there. But I read the passage again, and I'm convinced now that it was something he brought *from* the island! Can you think of anything here that could have come from there?"

Mrs Gunn smiled. "My goodness, Jupiter, how could I know that? I wasn't here, and I suppose he could have bought anything from that Cabrillo squire."

Jupiter nodded as if he hadn't really expected her to know.

"Try to think, ma'am," he said. "Meanwhile, I've thought of a whole new interpretation of old Angus's message. He says, *Follow my last course, read what my days built*. He says days, not day, and I think he means his *whole* course. *All* he did will add up to some message when we put it together. Like a jigsaw puzzle. We need all the pieces at once!"

"Wow!" Pete exclaimed. "That would explain why the ghost town and the island didn't tell us anything!"

Cluny said, "What's the next step then, Jupe?"

"There are two more steps, Cluny," Jupiter said, and took out the thin journal. "On November 21, 1872, Angus wrote, *Word from the Ortega* brothers that my order is now ready. I will need the large wagon. And the next day he wrote, *Returned from Rocky Beach with Ortega order. They do the best work, every piece the specified size—a miracle in this raw new land!* Then, until the next step, there are his usual laconic entries about 'work progressing'—plus two strange comments."

Jupiter looked up. "November 23—*Noted two strangers in area. Seafaring men.* And November 28 —*Strangers gone. To report to the Captain, I think.*"

"That's when he knew he was being watched," Bob said.

Jupiter nodded. "I can see him, fellows—alone out here, waiting for his wife and son. Unable to run, and maybe tired of running anyway. He had a premonition, perhaps, that he wasn't going to escape, so he decided to hide the treasure. There wasn't much time, so he used what he was building for Laura as a message to her."

"You said one more step to go?" Cluny reminded him.

Jupiter said, "On December 5 he wrote, *To Santa Barbara for last touch to Laura's surprise. Found a nice one, got it cheaply because establishment recently gutted by fire. One man's tragedy is often another man's fortune!* I wonder if Angus was thinking, when he wrote that, of the wreck and the treasure."

Jupiter closed the thin journal. "I looked up the Ortega brothers last night. They were well-known owners of a brick and stone yard in Rocky Beach, so Angus must have bought a load of bricks or stones for what he was building. There's still an Ortega Building Supplies Company, and perhaps they have records!"

"Then we'll go there!" Cluny cried.

"We will," Jupiter agreed, "but we'll split up and go to Santa Barbara, too. We know that Stebbins photographed the journal, so we've got to hurry now! Bob and Pete will go to the Ortega Company in Rocky Beach. Cluny and I will drive up to Santa Barbara with Hans. If we can discover what Angus bought up there, Cluny might recognise it."

"Is Uncle Titus going to let Hans drive you, First?" Bob asked.

"He will—as a favour to Mrs Gunn." Jupiter grinned. He turned to Cluny's mother. "If you could sell us some old stuff from your house, Mrs Gunn, and ask Hans to drive Cluny up to Santa Barbara as a favour."

Mrs Gunn laughed. "You have a devious mind, young man. But I'll do it; I have a few things your uncle might like. On one condition—you boys will carry this hibiscus out to the front for me! I was going to call Rory from the house, but since you're here you can help."

"We accept!" Jupiter said eagerly. "Come on, fellows."

The big redwood tub was very heavy, so they set it on two long two-by-fours that they found in the old stone shed. Each boy took an end of a two-by-four. Struggling, they carried the hibiscus round to the front of the house. As they set it down in place on the steps, they heard a car coming fast, and Professor Shay's station wagon drove up.

"I had to come and warn you, boys," Professor Shay said as he walked up quickly. "I reported young Stebbins to Chief Reynolds, and he checked the rascal's record. He was released on parole six months ago, and if he did break into your head-quarters, that is a parole violation! Stebbins knows that, boys, so he could be quite dangerous. Capture would mean return to prison!"

"Six months ago?" Pete said. "That's when the break-ins started here, Jupe!"

"Yes, Second, it is," Jupiter agreed grimly. "I think—" He stopped, his eyes suddenly alert. He sniffed at the air. "Fellows? Do you smell something? I—"

Pete sniffed. "Smoke! Something's burning!"

"It's from behind the house!" Cluny cried.

They ran to the corner of the house. After a moment they saw it—smoke billowing from the old stone shed.

"The shed's on fire, boys!" Mrs Gunn exclaimed.

All at once Jupiter began to feel the pockets of his jacket and to pat at his trousers. He looked at his hands as if surprised that he wasn't holding something. Panic filled his eyes.

"The journal!" The First Investigator said in despair. "I put it down when we carried the tub! It must be in the shed!"

13

A Wild Pursuit

THEY RAN to the old shed. The smoke was thicker now, but there were no flames reaching outside. The stone shed wouldn't burn easily.

"Only the timber inside is burning!" Pete yelled.

Cluny ran up with a fire extinguisher. Pete and Bob tore off their jackets and, with Cluny leading the way, carefully entered the burning shed.

"It's all in the loose timber pile!" Cluny cried.

Outside, Jupiter, Mrs Gunn, and Professor Shay listened to the sounds of the fire extinguisher and of jackets beating at the flames inside. Moments later the smoke thinned, and then all but stopped. Pete came out triumphant. He held the thin journal.

"Barely singed, Jupe!" the Second Investigator crowed. "Lucky, too, because it was very near the fire."

Jupiter took the journal and flipped through the pages to be sure they were all right.

Suddenly they became aware of someone running towards them. It was Rory! He was shouting and pointing off behind the stone shed.

"O'er tha' way! The rear o' the shed! I saw him, ye fools! Watching he was, no' a minute ago!"

"We can stop him!" Professor Shay cried.

They all ran past the shed towards the thick brush and trees at the end of the valley. Rory was in the lead.

"There! In wi' the trees!" Rory shouted. "Making for the high road he is!"

Spread out, they all plunged in among the trees, crashing through the heavy brush. Professor Shay was over to the right in an attempt to head off the escaping arsonist. Rory was somewhere up ahead. Jupiter and Bob, bringing up the rear, stopped a moment to scan the dense undergrowth under the grey-green live-oaks.

There was a sudden silence, as if everyone had stopped the chase to listen. Up ahead a voice muttered that the scoundrel was hiding. Jupiter and Bob began to move cautiously on again. They went some fifty yards in the shadowed brush and trees. Something snapped in the brush!

"Bob!" Jupiter whispered, peering around.

The cry came right by Jupiter. A figure leaped out of the brush, and Jupiter went down in a tangle of arms and legs and loud yells.

"I've got him! Fellows! I've got him!" Pete called.

"Help!" Jupiter echoed.

"Pete!" Bob groaned. "It's us! You've got Jupe."

Jupiter blinked up at Pete on top of him. "What?"

"Ulp," Pete said. "I thought . . . I mean I heard . . ."

"Get off me!" Jupiter said, struggling to get up. He brushed at his clothes. "Try to look before you jump, Second."

Pete grinned. "Well, you thought I was the criminal too, didn't you?"

"Boy, did you two look funny!" Bob said.

All three Investigators were laughing when Professor Shay, Rory, and Cluny came slowly back and found them. The professor's eyes jumped with anger behind his rimless glasses. His round pink face was almost comic with frustrated fury. Rory glowered.

"Got clean away, blast him," the Scotsman said. "I saw him clear, though. That Java Jim it was, from the way you've told about him."

"Stebbins, you mean, McNab," Professor Shay disagreed. "I saw—"

"Ye're daft, man!" Rory snapped. "I saw the beard 'n all the sailor garb the boys described!"

"Moustache, you mean," Professor Shay insisted. "That black hair must have—"

"Don't ye think I'd know that Stebbins having seen him?"

"But—!" Professor Shay began, and then seemed to think. "Well, I could be mistaken, I suppose. You saw better than my glimpse."

"That indeed I did," Rory said. "I ha' nae doubts."

"Then," Jupiter said urgently, "there's no time to lose! If Java Jim tried to destroy the journal, it can only mean one thing—he thinks he knows all he needs to find the treasure! We'll have to move fast now. Come on, men!"

Jupiter led the way back through the dense brush to the massive old house. Mrs Gunn stood waiting anxiously. Hans was with her, having left the truck to investigate all the excitement.

"The vandal escaped," Rory growled. "If I'd come from the house a minute sooner, I'd ha' collared him."

"You were in the house, Mr McNab?" Jupiter asked.

"That I was, boy. Smelled the smoke."

"Arson should be reported," Professor Shay said. "I only came to warn you about young Stebbins being a parole violator, and now I must get back. But I'll stop at the police station and report Java Jim and this latest outrage."

"Ay, ye better," Rory agreed. The surly Scotsman's voice was grudgingly friendly. "It's an apology I may be owing ye, boys. I'm not saying there is any treasure, but I know now that others besides ye yersel's think there is." Rory shook his head. "Dangerous men, I'm thinking. For the police to handle. It's no' a job for boys."

Professor Shay nodded. "I'm afraid I must agree, boys."

"Perhaps—" Mrs Gunn began doubtfully.

"We're not in any danger, ma'am," Jupiter said quickly. "It's obvious that Java Jim thinks he has all he needs. He didn't try to attack us. And at the island, Stebbins ran away. It's the treasure they want, and our best course is to find it first! Bob and Pete are careful, and Cluny and I will have Hans with us."

"I'm still no' liking it," Rory insisted.

"I'm sure the boys will be responsible," Mrs Gunn said quietly. "They're old enough now."

"Thanks, Mum!" Cluny beamed.

Professor Shay smiled. "I have faith in their judgment too, Mrs Gunn. Now I must attend to my duties. But keep me informed, eh, boys?"

The little professor returned to his station wagon and drove off. Rory reluctantly helped Hans load the truck with the items Mrs Gunn was letting Uncle Titus have. Then he walked towards Mrs Gunn's old Ford.

"Ye all may ha' time to waste, but not I," Rory said grumpily. "That fire burned the small generator in the shed. I'll ha' to go to ha' it repaired."

Rory drove the Ford back to the burned shed, and Bob and Pete got their bikes from the truck to ride to Rocky Beach.

"Look sharply," Jupiter admonished them before they rode away. "These are the last two steps of old Angus's course!"

Then Jupiter and Cluny climbed into the truck, and Hans started north for Santa Barbara.

14

Java Jim Again

JUPITER FIDGETED on the seat of the truck as they drove north for Santa Barbara.

"Faster, Hans," he urged. "We must get there first!"

"We get there in good time, Jupe," Hans said placidly. "Hurry too much, maybe we don't get there at all."

Jupiter sat back chewing on his lip. Cluny, who had been looking at old Angus's second journal, looked up in confusion.

"Jupiter, I just noticed this entry for Santa Barbara doesn't say *where* Angus went! Where do we go when we get there?"

Hans grunted. "Santa Barbara is big town."

"Big enough to have well-kept records," Jupiter said a little smugly. "We're going to find where Angus went by using the one important fact he did give us."

"What's that Jupe?" Cluny asked.

"That he bought something at a shop that had recently been gutted by fire!" Jupiter said triumphantly. "In 1872 Santa Barbara was small enough for the newspaper to write about any local fire!"

They reached the lush outskirts of Santa Barbara

D

in mid-afternoon and found the imitation-Moorish building of the Santa Barbara *Sun-Press* on De La Guerre Plaza. The receptionist sent them to a Mr Pidgeon on the second floor. The editor was a thin, smiling man.

"In 1872?" Mr Pidgeon said. "No, we weren't in existence then. There was a local paper, though, and you're right, young man, a fire would have been reported."

"Where would we find the old paper's morgue, sir?" Jupiter asked.

"Well, we took over all its assets and files," Mr Pidgeon said, "but, unfortunately, all records before 1900 were lost in an earthquake and fire."

Jupiter groaned. "All the records, Mr Pidgeon?"

"I'm afraid so," the editor said. He thought for a moment. "However, there might be a way. I know an old writer who worked on that paper over sixty years ago. I'm not sure, but I think he kept a private morgue on the old paper. Sort of a hobby."

"Is he in Santa Barbara now, sir?" Jupiter exclaimed.

"He certainly is," and Mr Pidgeon opened a small, revolving address file on his desk. "His name's Jesse Widmer, and he lives at 1600 Anacapa Street. I'm sure he'd be glad to see you boys."

In the truck again, they drove up to the 1600 block of Anacapa Street. Number 1600 was a small adobe house set at the end of a long walk, behind a larger house. Jupiter and Cluny hastened up the walk while Hans remained in the truck. Jupiter stopped suddenly on the path.

A door had slammed somewhere, and feet ran away behind the small adobe.

"Look, Jupe!" Cluny pointed.

The front door of the small house stood ajar. As they stood listening, a weak cry came from the adobe.

"Help!" And then louder, "Help me!"

"Someone's in trouble in there!" cried Jupe and dashed forward with Cluny. Hans leaped out of the truck and sprinted after them.

The adobe's front door opened on to a small, neat living-room lined with books and framed front pages of old newspapers.

"Please! Help!"

The cry came from an inner room on the left. The boys followed it into a study, crammed with stacks of ancient newspapers and magazines. A typewriter stood on a desk with typed pages in a box beside it, as if someone were writing a book.

An old man lay on the floor. His glazed eyes rolled up at the boys. Blood trickled from his mouth, and his face was cut.

"*Mein Gott*," swore Hans when he saw the old man. He lifted the writer up gently and helped him into an easy-chair. Cluny got a glass of water. The old man drank thirstily.

"A bearded man," the old man said. "With a scarred face, wearing a pea-jacket. Who . . . who are you?"

"Java Jim!" Cluny exclaimed.

Jupiter told the old man who they were. "Mr Pidgeon at the *Sun-Press* sent us to you, sir. If you're Jesse Widmer."

"I am." The old man nodded. "Java Jim? That's the man who attacked me?"

"Yes, sir," Jupiter said. "What did he want, Mr Widmer?"

Mr Widmer took deep breaths as Hans gently tended his cuts, smiling to show that his injuries weren't serious.

"He didn't come recommended by anybody at the *Sun-Press*. Just barged in here. Wanted to know about a fire in some store in 1872, around November," the old man said. "The *Argyll Queen* treasure—you say that bearded man wants it? There *is* a treasure?"

"You're interested in the *Argyll Queen* treasure?" Cluny said.

Jesse Widmer nodded. "Have been for a long time. Studied it for years, got a lot of clippings in my private morgue."

"What did you tell Java Jim, sir?" Jupiter asked.

"Nothing. Didn't like him. So he hit me and searched my files. Found what he wanted, I guess, and ran out," the old man said. "Took a clipping with him."

Jupiter groaned. "He took a clipping, sir? What did it say? It's important, sir."

Jesse Widmer shook his injured head. "Don't know, but I can find out if you want."

"You can, sir?" Cluny cried. "Would you try?"

"Do more than try," Jesse Widmer said. "Got all my files on microfilm. Hand me that box on my desk."

Cluny handed the long, narrow box to Mr Widmer. The old man went through it and drew out a box of microfilm. "Here's 1872. Put it on that reading machine over there."

Jupiter sat down at the viewer and started reading the filmed clippings, beginning with September 1872. He turned the spool slowly.

"Here's something!" the First Investigator cried. "November 15! Wright and Sons, Ship Chandlers, suffered a serious fire which gutted their storehouse. That must be it!"

"What's a ship chandler?" asked Cluny.

"A retail dealer who sells supplies and equipment for ships," answered Jupe.

"Wright and Sons?" Mr Widmer said. "They're still in business. Down near the harbour."

"Then let's hurry!" Cluny urged.

Hans said, "I think we must call a doctor for Mr Widmer."

The old man shook his head. "No, no! I'm all right. I'll call my own doctor. You stop that bearded man. That's the best medicine I can get now. Go on, go on!"

Jupiter hesitated only for a moment. Then he grinned at Mr Widmer, and hurried out with Cluny and Hans. Hans drove downtown towards the harbour. They found the old-fashioned shop of Wright and Sons, Ship Chandlers on a side street not far from the water.

An elderly gentleman greeted them. "May I help you?"

"Do you have records back to 1872?" Cluny burst out.

Jupiter said, "We're trying to find out—"

"If you are friends of that bearded ruffian who was just here," the elderly man said stiffly, "you march right out!"

"We're not his friends, sir," Jupiter said, and explained briefly about their search.

"Angus Gunn, eh?" the old man said. "Alas, as I told that rude man, the earthquake destroyed all our older records."

Jupiter was crestfallen. "Then there's no way we can find out what Angus Gunn bought here back in 1872?"

The elderly man shook his head. "Unless . . . wait here. Browse through our stock, I may be five or ten minutes."

The elderly man went up some stairs to a door marked "Private." Hans, who loved unusual objects as much as Uncle Titus did, began to inspect all the marine wares. Cluny went to the front of the shop to study a ship model while Jupiter waited impatiently. Suddenly Cluny stared out of the store window.

"Jupiter!" the red-headed boy whispered urgently.

Jupiter hurried up. "What, Cluny?"

"Someone was out there watching the store!"

"Where?" Jupiter's eyes searched the street.

"At the far end of the street! When I looked at

him, he jumped behind that last building. Maybe it's Java Jim!"

Jupiter glanced to the back of the shop. The elderly man hadn't reappeared, and Hans was absorbed in an old ship's clock. Jupiter beckoned to Cluny, and they went outside.

"Let's see if we can spot him," Jupiter said.

They walked watchfully towards the harbour, keeping close to the buildings. At the corner they peered round. Cluny cried softly:

"Jupiter! A green Volkswagen!"

The small car was parked on the other side of the broad harbour street. Beyond it, Jupiter saw a small, moustached youth hurrying across an area of wet sand to an old wooden barge that was beached at the edge of the water.

"It's not Java Jim, it's Stebbins!" Jupiter exclaimed. They watched the wild-haired youth disappear behind the partially buried barge, his mouth moving as if talking. "He's meeting someone, Cluny!"

"Java Jim, maybe?" Cluny guessed.

"Follow me," Jupiter said grimly.

The stout leader of the Investigators walked across the street and approached the barge from the side.

"If it is Java Jim and Stebbins," Jupiter whispered, "maybe we can hear them. Find out what they're planning. And I'd like to know how Java Jim knew to go directly to Jesse Widmer."

He motioned Cluny to silence and stopped at

the barge, listening hard. But there was no sound from the other side.

"It's too far," Cluny whispered. "Let's look round the other side."

"No," said Jupe. "We might run into them. We'll spy on them from above."

He pointed to a ladder on the side of the barge. It was a little difficult to climb, as the barge lay tilted lengthwise on a slope down to the water. Jupe managed to hoist himself up, and Cluny followed. Close together, they stepped lightly across the deck towards the far side—and with a ripping of rotten wood the deck gave way. They plummeted down into a black hole!

"Oooooff!" Jupiter grunted, buried in something soft and wet.

"Old sacks," Cluny gasped. "We fell on a pile of sacks!"

When they had caught their breath, they stood up on the sloping floor and looked around. They were in the hold of the barge, a dark, slimy place with a half-rotted bottom. A little light came from some chinks in the old wooden sides—and from the jagged opening in a hatch where they had fallen through. The hatch was twelve feet above them!

"Look for something to stand on," Jupiter said.

They walked round the slippery hold. Except for the sacks it was bare. No boxes, or boards, or ropes, or ladders! Something small scuttled in a dark corner. Rats!

Cluny looked at Jupiter. "There's no way out, Jupe!"

"Let's check again! From end to end!" Jupiter urged.

They walked all the way down the sloping bottom of the barge—and stood at the edge of water. Jupiter gulped.

"Cluny, look at the walls," he quavered. "There's a high water mark on them. When . . . when the tide comes in, this leaky hold is almost under water!"

They hurried back to stand beneath the hatch they had fallen through.

"Start yelling!" Cluny said.

A shadow fell across the jagged opening above, and a face peered down at them. A young face with a moustache!

"Don't waste your breath," Stebbins said grimly. "No one comes here much in winter, and no one on the street will hear you over the traffic."

They stared up at the driver of the green Volkswagen. His eyes flashed down at them. "I want to talk to you kids!"

15

A Slip of the Tongue

ON THEIR bikes, Bob and Pete reached the Ortega Building Supplies yard in mid-afternoon. A dark-faced man was loading bricks on a truck. When the boys told him they wanted to ask some questions about the old Ortega brothers, he wiped the sweat from his brow and grinned.

"*Si*, the famous Ortega brothers! The best stone masons in all California in the old days. My great-grandfather and great-granduncle. I am Emiliano Ortega." The smiling man sighed loudly. "Now I am the best stone mason, but today no one wants the best stonework. Too expensive."

"Then you know all about the old Ortega brothers?" Bob said.

"Sure. What do you want to know, *muchachos*?"

"They sold a wagonload of something to a Mr Angus Gunn on November 22, 1872. We want to know what they sold."

"*Caramba!*" Emiliano Ortega cried. "You want to know what someone bought in 1872? A hundred years ago?"

"Is it too long ago?" Pete asked.

"You can't help us?" Bob said in dismay.

"A hundred years!" Mr Ortega said in horror, and then he laughed, his black eyes twinkling. "Sure I can help you! The Ortegas keep the best records in the state. Come."

Mr Ortega took them into the yard office and went to an old wooden filing cabinet. He rummaged in the back of it among yellowed folders. At last he drew out a file, blew dust from it with a grin at the boys, and opened it on his desk.

"You said November 22, Angus Gunn. Okay, let's see what we—here it is! *Angus Gunn, Phantom Lake, on special order: one ton of cut granite, paid in cash and carried away.*"

"A ton of granite?" Pete said. "What kind of granite? I mean, what kind of stones?"

Mr Ortega shook his head. "It doesn't say—just the weight of stone. It was a special order, and judging by the price it wasn't just ordinary rock, but that's all I know."

"What kind of special orders could there have been back then, Mr Ortega?" Bob asked. "What *was* a special order?"

"Well." Mr Ortega rubbed at his jaw. "A special order would have meant something more than just loose stone from our quarry. A special size of stones, or shape, or maybe finish. Some work done on the stone after it was quarried, eh? Even polished. But this order wasn't polished stone— too cheap. Did this Angus Gunn maybe build a sidewalk?"

"Sidewalk?" Pete gaped.

"They used stone for that in those days—big, flat stones."

"Not that we know of," Bob said.

"Well, then it could be any size of stone, big or small. For a house, a foundation, flagstones, a wall, anything." Mr Ortega shrugged. "Is the size and shape important, kids?"

"Yes, sir!" they cried together.

Mr Ortega nodded. "Okay, there's an order number on the sales slip. The stone would have come from our old quarry out in the hills. We don't use it much now—only keep a caretaker there—and the specification sheet for that old order might still be lying around the quarry office."

"Gosh," Bob cried, "can we go there?"

"Sure," Mr Ortega said, and told them where the quarry was.

"Why, it's only a couple of miles past Phantom Lake!" Bob exclaimed. "We'll see if Jupe and Cluny are back before we go!"

But at that moment Jupe and Cluny were staring up at the moustached face of Stebbins. The wild-haired young man peered down through the hatch.

"We're not talking to you!" Cluny declared stoutly, looking up. "We know who you are!"

Above, Stebbins's face seemed alarmed. "What do you know?"

"We know you're a thief that Professor Shay had to send to prison," Jupiter said hotly, "and you've broken your parole to steal Angus Gunn's treasure!"

"The police know it, too!" Cluny said.

Stebbins lifted his head and looked round the deck. Then he glared down at the boys again.

"So Professor Shay told you that, did he?" Stebbins said. "How come you kids are working with Shay?"

"He's working with us," Jupiter corrected him. "We found the second journal, the one you photographed!"

"You found—" Stebbins hesitated. "What did you learn in that store over there?"

"You think we'd tell you?" Cluny said.

"Why not ask your partner, Java Jim?" Jupiter countered.

"Java Jim? What do you kids know about him?"

"We know you're both after the treasure!" Cluny cried. "But you won't steal it! We'll beat you to—"

"Beat me to it?" Stebbins broke in. "Then you don't know where it is yet, do you? Professor Shay doesn't know? But you think that Java Jim does know?"

"Maybe Java Jim hasn't told you all he knows," Jupiter said, and smiled. "No honour among thieves, Stebbins!"

"Thieves?" Stebbins repeated. "If I told—" He stopped, shook his head. "No, you wouldn't—"

The wild-haired young man stared down at them for another moment. Then his eyes flashed again.

"There're four of you. Where are the other two?"

"Wouldn't you like to know!" Cluny taunted him.

Jupiter laughed. "We told you we'd beat you!"

"Beat me?" Stebbins said again, and suddenly he smiled. "So, they're on the last step, right? The Ortega stone yard, that's where they are! Thanks, kids."

Jupiter groaned. He'd told Stebbins where Bob and Pete were! The young man smiled down, and then vanished. They heard him hurry across the deck above, jump down to the sand, and walk quickly away.

Alone, Jupiter and Cluny watched the tide rising in the hold. There was no way out. They began to yell.

It was late afternoon when Bob and Pete biked up to Phantom Lake Lodge once more. Mrs Gunn came out to greet them.

"No, Jupiter and Cluny aren't back yet, boys," she said.

They told her what they had learned at the Ortega yard.

"A ton of special stone?" Mrs Gunn mused. "Heavens, what for, boys? The foundation of this house, perhaps?"

"No, ma'am. The house was already built," Pete pointed out.

"Can you think of anything else here built of stone?" Bob asked.

Mrs Gunn thought, and shook her head. "Not a thing, boys."

"There has to be something!" Pete insisted. "Old Angus must—"

They heard a vehicle coming fast up the road from the highway. The truck? Then they saw it —Mrs Gunn's Ford. It sped down to the house and Rory jumped out. He carried the small generator he'd gone to have repaired.

"There's nae a mon to do decent work these days," the Scotsman grumbled. "Kept me waiting a' afternoon for the repairs!"

"Rory," Mrs Gunn said, "do you remember anything built here out of stone? A whole ton of stone? Aside from the house and shed?"

"Stone?" Rory frowned. "A ton o' it?"

Bob and Pete repeated what Mr Ortega had told them.

"I dinna recall anything," Rory said. "Ye say the quarry might tell ye more o' the size 'n shape o' the stones?"

Bob nodded. "But it's getting late. We'd never make it on our bikes before dark."

"Then I'll drive ye there," Rory said. "I ha' another trip I could make in that direction. I'll drop ye on my way, and ye can ride yer bikes back."

Bob put his bike in the boot of the Ford, and Pete squeezed his in along the back seat. They jumped in the front beside Rory and drove off.

There was still light when they reached the

entrance to the old quarry. Rory dropped them and their bikes, and drove away.

The old quarry was a deep, vast pit at least two hundred yards across, with some water at the bottom. Stone jutted everywhere, glowing in the sunset. The whole mountainside had been gouged out in a series of encircling terraces, like steps. Far across, the quarry opened out away from the mountain and was only a few terraces deep. Here, near the bottom, a sturdy shack stood on a stone terrace that gave directly on to a low shoulder of the mountain. There was light in the shack, and a truck parked by it.

"The caretaker's still here!" Pete said.

They scrambled down into the quarry and made their way along a terrace. They were less than halfway to the shack when the light went out. A man came out and got into the truck.

They shouted, "Hey! . . . Mister! . . ."

The man was too far away, and the truck engine drowned their voices. They ran, but the truck drove off on a back road and was gone. When they reached the shack, it was dark and padlocked.

"Too late," Pete moaned.

Bob studied the shack. Its four windows were shuttered and locked outside by heavy boards in slots. "Maybe we can get in and find the records ourselves. Mr Ortega knows we're here."

Pete unbarred a shutter. "Bob! This window's not locked!"

"We're in luck," Bob said. "Come on."

They climbed inside. The shack was an office with old wooden files and furniture. Pete found a cabinet labelled " 1870–1900". He opened it, flipped through the files, and took out a folder marked " 1872". He carried it to a desk. Bob leaned over his shoulder.

Light footsteps sounded outside the shack.

"What's that?" Bob whirled.

The open shutter banged closed. They heard the board slide in place to lock it. Footsteps hurried away.

They were prisoners!

16

A Sound in the Night

THE LATE sun slanted across the ragged opening in the hatch. Jupiter and Cluny had shouted themselves hoarse. Now they sat against the dank wall at the upper end of the barge and watched the tide rising steadily towards them.

"How long do you think we have, Jupiter?" Cluny said quietly.

"Perhaps two hours more," Jupiter said. "Someone will find us soon."

"No one's heard us yet," Cluny said in a low voice.

"They will. Hans must have missed us long ago."

"But he doesn't know we're in this barge. He'll never look here!"

"In a few minutes we'll start yelling again. Someone will hear us."

"Sure, of course they will," Cluny said doubtfully.

But after a few more minutes, Jupiter didn't start to shout. Instead, his eyes seemed to stare at something.

"Cluny," the First Investigator said, "that locker over there. It's attached to the wall, but maybe we can pry it loose. The wood looks rotten."

Cluny shook his head. "It's too low to climb on and reach the hatch, Jupiter."

"Not to climb on, to float on!" Jupiter said. "If we can get it loose, and it floats, we could hang on to it and float up with the tide!"

They both jumped up and sloshed through the rising water to the locker. It was built into the side of the hold and nailed to the floor. The boys looked about for anything to pry the locker up with.

A heavy tread sounded on the deck above. A slow step, as if wary and careful not to be heard!

"Jupiter!" Cluny cried, "someone's up—"

"Shhhhh!" Jupiter warned. "No way of knowing who it is, Cluny. We haven't been yelling for a while. No one could have heard us and come looking."

Cluny nodded nervously. Both boys held their breath and listened. The heavy tread moved on cautiously across the deck towards the broken boards of the hatch. Then the steps stopped. There was a silence.

"Jupiter?" a deep voice called down. "Cluny?"

It was Hans!

"Hans!" Jupiter yelled. "Down here!"

The boys waded over to stand under the jagged opening in the hatch.

"Get us out of here!" Cluny called up.

"I get you out. Wait," Hans said from above.

They heard him walk across the deck, and then there was a ripping of wood. Moments later the ladder from the side of the barge was lowered down. Jupe and Cluny scrambled up to the deck.

"Boy," Cluny said, "are we glad to see you, Hans!"

"I look everywhere for you when you are missing from store," Hans said solemnly. "You should not go off without me."

"How did you find us?" Jupiter asked.

"I look through streets, ice cream places, everywhere," Hans said. "When I go back to chandler shop, a boy is there who tells me he saw you on barge so, I come here."

"A boy saw us?" Jupiter said, frowning.

"Why didn't he help us himself, then?" Cluny wondered.

"Yes," Jupiter said thoughtfully. "Is he still at the shop?"

"No, he has left. He showed me barge, and ran off," Hans said. "I forgot. Mr Wright have a message for you. He went to talk to his father, very old man. Old Mr Wright says no way to tell what Angus Gunn bought in 1872, but there is one way back at Gunn Lodge."

"What way?" Jupiter asked eagerly.

"Old man say *all* things sold from store in those days have brass plate on them with name of Wright and Sons," Hans said. "You must look for brass plate on something."

"Jupiter," Cluny urged, "let's get home and look!"

"And fast," Jupiter said. "I forgot something,

too. Stebbins knows where Pete and Bob went! They may be in danger!"

Christmas tree lights were shining through the windows of the lodge into the early night as Hans parked the truck in the drive. Cluny and Jupiter jumped out and ran inside. Hans followed more slowly, and went to phone Uncle Titus and report. Mrs Gunn was standing in the living-room. She was alone with a roaring fire against the night chill.

"Mum!" Cluny blurted out as they ran in. "Do we have anything with a brass plate on it marked 'Wright and Sons'?" He told her what they'd learned in Santa Barbara.

"You couldn't find out what old Angus bought?" Mrs Gunn said, knitting her brows. "A brass plate? Well, many of Angus's old things have brass plates—it was common in those days. But I don't recall anything labelled 'Wright and Sons'."

"Think, Mum, please!" Cluny urged.

Jupiter asked, "Have Bob and Pete come back?"

"Yes. They returned here to tell me about old Angus buying a ton of granite stones from the Ortegas," Mrs Gunn said. "But they didn't know what kind of stone, or what size and shape, so Rory drove them to the old Ortega quarry, and then went off on some errand. But—"

"They're not back yet?" Jupiter said, and glanced at the grandfather clock. It was almost seven o'clock.

"No, and neither is Rory," Mrs Gunn said. "But—"

A strange sound came suddenly through the night. From somewhere outside, behind the house, far away. Hans came into the large living-room and stopped to listen with the others.

It was a sound like distant hammering. With a hollow ring, like metal against stone.

"There!" Mrs Gunn said. "That's what I've been trying to tell you, boys. I've been hearing that sound in the night for over an hour. It frightens me. What could it be?"

"Sounds like someone knocking down a wall," Hans said.

"A wall? But no one lives that close to us. There's nothing in that direction except—" Mrs Gunn stopped.

"Except what, Mum?" Cluny asked. "I don't know anything out that way."

"Perhaps you've never seen it. There's an old smokehouse out back. It hasn't been used since your father was a boy. I'd forgotten all about it."

"A smokehouse?" Jupiter said. "A *stone* smokehouse?"

"Why, I suppose it could be stone. It was covered with vines when I first saw it, and I never looked closely."

"Hans!" Jupiter cried. "Get the lantern from the truck."

Hans got the electric lantern, and Mrs Gunn led them back through the brush along an old, overgrown path. The December night was cold for Southern California. The path went on for almost half a mile, finally passing an old wooden cabin.

"A worker's cabin from Grandfather Gunn's day," Mrs Gunn explained. "That's why the smokehouse was out here."

"Did old Angus build the smokehouse, ma'am?" Jupiter asked.

"I'm not sure. I rather thought Grandfather Gunn did—Angus's son." She peered into the dark. "It should be just about here."

The sound of hammering had ceased. Mrs Gunn led the others off the path into the heavy brush— brush that was all torn and trampled. They pushed through to the smokehouse—and found nothing but a pile of stones!

"Someone's knocked it down!" Mrs Gunn said.

"Looking for the treasure!" Cluny exclaimed.

"I suppose we have Stebbins to thank for this," said Jupiter. "Maybe Java Jim, too. Both of them could have returned from Santa Barbara hours ago. Though how they could have known about this smokehouse . . . ?"

Hans picked up a sledge hammer. "Handle is still warm from hands."

They listened hard, but there was no sound in the night. Jupiter examined the remains of the smokehouse closely in the light of the lantern.

"The walls were apparently solid stone," he said slowly. "And from the looks of the firebrick inside, I don't think anything was hidden inside the firebox. Spiders all over, too." He looked all around. "No sign of anything dragged off."

Cluny was pawing among the scattered stones. "Jupe! Here's a stone with writing on it!"

Hans carried the lantern over. Jupiter brushed dirt away from the stone and read, "C. Gunn, 1883."

"Grandfather Gunn. His name was Cluny, too," Mrs Gunn said.

Jupiter grinned. "Then old Angus didn't build the smokehouse. The treasure couldn't have been in it. Let's go back to the house."

When they reached the lodge, Professor Shay's station wagon was parked in front next to the truck. The professor himself was shivering on the steps, blue from cold in his light suit.

"Too cold for California," the professor said, and then grinned. "I came to see what you found out today, boys. Tell me now, quickly."

In the warm living-room with its roaring fire and Christmas tree, Jupiter told the professor what they had learned in Santa Barbara.

"A brass plate? And Java Jim and Stebbins were both there?" The professor pondered. "Have you found the brass plate here?"

"Not yet, sir," Cluny said. "We haven't really looked."

"We're waiting for Bob and Pete," Jupiter explained. He related Bob and Pete's trip to the Ortega yard and the quarry, and looked uneasily at the clock. "Rory drove them, but . . . Wait, here they are now!"

The Ford drove up outside. Rory got out and

strode into the house rubbing his hands. He was alone.

"Where are Bob and Pete?" Mrs Gunn wanted to know.

"Where I left them at the quarry, I've nae doubt," Rory snapped. He looked at Cluny. "And what did ye find on yer wild-goose chase to Santa Barbara?"

Cluny told him hurriedly. "We haven't looked for the brass plate here yet because Bob and Pete aren't back, and because someone knocked down the old smokehouse at the back."

"Smokehouse?" Rory scowled. "Ay, I'd forgot about that." Now Rory looked at the clock. "Those boys aren't back yet? They should ha' been back o'er an hour ago."

"A *stone* smokehouse?" Professor Shay said, alarmed. "But how would someone know about Old Angus's load of stones unless—"

"They talked to Pete and Bob," Cluny said.

"Or visited the Ortega yard," Jupiter added. He explained how he had tipped off Stebbins. "What worries me now," he went on grimly, "is that Stebbins and Java Jim could have learned about the old quarry, too. One of them might have followed Pete and Bob there!"

"What!" Professor Shay started for the door. "Then Bob and Pete may be in trouble, boys— even hurt somewhere! Hurry!"

The men and boys ran to the cars.

17

The Last Clue

THE OLD quarry gleamed faintly silver in the cold starlight, its depths fading into bottomless dark. They parked at the entrance where Rory had left Bob and Pete. There was no light anywhere in the quarry.

"Look for some trail!" Jupiter said.

They fanned out at the top of the quarry. Rory soon found the bikes.

"Just where I left 'em," the Scotsman said grimly. "They must ha' gone down into the quarry. Anywhere else, they'd ha' taken 'em."

Carefully they all clambered down into the quarry. Their flashlights made the terraces look like some giant's stairs. The water in the bottom eerily reflected the flashlight beams. Professor Shay looked at the dank water far below.

"If they slipped," the professor said with a shudder. "All the way down—?"

"Don't even talk about it, Professor," Cluny quavered.

Jupiter looked along the high stone sides of the terraces for chalked question-mark signs. There were none he could see.

"If they were being followed," Jupiter said,

"they didn't know it. If they had, they would have left question-mark signs to show me their escape route. We always carry our chalk."

"I'm not sure that's good, Jupiter," Professor Shay said. "It could mean they were taken by surprise."

No one said anything to that grim thought. In silence, they continued on along a terrace halfway down the old quarry. They played their flashlights and lanterns up and down. All they saw were the stone terraces, twisted old trees clinging to the walls in crevices, and piles of fallen rock.

Small animals scurried in the dark, and twice snakes slithered across their path and under piles of stone. Far off coyotes bayed. Some large bird flew heavily through the trees up at the rim of the quarry. A hunting bird, a horned owl, searching for prey.

Still there was no sign of Bob or Pete, and no sounds in the night except the animals. They had almost completely circled the quarry to the far side when they heard the sudden noise!

"Listen!" Hans whispered.

Something metal had jangled not far ahead.

"Can you see?" Cluny whispered.

"No," Professor Shay muttered.

Wood scraped against wood and metal.

"There!" Jupiter exclaimed softly. "A shack is down there!"

In his excitement his voice rose higher than he had intended. There was a clatter down by the shack, and someone ran. Rory shone his flashlight.

The beam picked out a thin figure running towards a small car parked near the shack.

"It's Stebbins!" Professor Shay cried. "Stop him this time!"

"Bob! Pete!" Jupiter called.

"Head him off, ye fools!" Rory raged.

"Stebbins! Halt!" Professor Shay yelled.

The slender young man reached his green Volkswagen, jumped in, and roared off down a back dirt road before they could even reach the dark shack.

"He escaped!" Professor Shay cried bitterly. "The villain!"

Jupiter wasn't worried about Stebbins. "But where are Bob and Pete? What's he done to them?"

Cluny swallowed hard, and the men stood silent. Jupiter stared round in the dark.

"Bob! Pete!" he called.

His voice echoed off the high walls of the quarry, ghostly in the night. The echo seemed to go on and on and changed suddenly into a different sound:

"Help! Jupe! We're in here!"

They all froze.

"It's them!" Cluny cried.

The voices came again. "Jupe! In here!"

"Look!" Professor Shay said. "A light in the shack!"

Cracks of light had suddenly appeared in the old shack, outlining a door and windows. Jupe scrambled down to the terrace the shack was on, followed by the others. He ran to the door and started rattling the padlock. From inside, Pete yelled,

"The front window, First! Unbar the shutter!"

Rory jumped to the window, removed the bar that held the shutters closed, and threw them open. Bob and Pete grinned out.

"Boy," Pete said, "we thought we were stuck here for the night—or worse."

"Someone was trying to come in after us!" Bob exclaimed. "That's why we had the lights out. He tried the padlock, then he started to unbar the shutters."

"Stebbins, the scoundrel!" Professor Shay said.

"He must a' locked you in there," Rory decided. "Was coming back for who kens what devilment when we scared him off."

"Come out, boys," Hans said.

Bob shook his head. "No, you climb in! We've got the last clue in here!"

Excited, they all climbed in one by one. Hans could barely fit in through the window. Inside the small office, Bob and Pete showed them the file folder open on the desk.

"*Special order number 143*," Jupiter read aloud. "*For A. Gunn, ship to yard, ten square-cut matched monument stones. Granite.*" Jupiter looked up. "Ten monument stones?"

"Adding up to a ton of stone," Pete said. "Two hundred pounds a stone. What did old Angus want with ten big stones? Did he build some kind of monument?"

Jupiter shook his head in bewilderment.

"There's nae a monument at Phantom Lake," Rory said.

"Perhaps somewhere else?" Professor Shay asked.

"A monument built for Laura in some town?" Cluny guessed.

"No," Jupiter said slowly. "I'm convinced Laura's surprise is at Phantom Lake—somewhere. The journal couldn't mean anything else the way Angus wrote it. He always came *home* to work on Laura's surprise."

"Then whatever he built, boys," Professor Shay said, "is hidden! It must be that. Hidden at Phantom Lake so cleverly that no one has ever

"Or," Bob said, "so obvious we just don't see it! stumbled over it!" Maybe we look at it all the time, like Poe's purloined letter, and don't see it because it's right in front of us!"

"There must be something we don't yet know," Professor Shay said bitterly.

"There's one thing I know," Pete said. "I know it's late, and I'm hungry. Let's go home and eat, fellows."

They all laughed.

"Let's eat at my house, guys," Cluny urged. "You can call your folks. Mum makes a swell dinner, and we can try to puzzle it all out!"

"That sounds like a sensible suggestion." Professor Shay smiled. "If Mrs Gunn doesn't mind feeding an over-age treasure-hunter."

"I know she won't, Professor," Cluny said.

They made their way back round the quarry and up to the bikes and cars. Bob and Pete loaded their bikes into the truck, and all four boys got into the back. As they drove off, Pete suddenly spoke once more.

"I know something else, too, First," he said to Jupiter. "You said this case was maybe like a jigsaw puzzle—*all* the pieces go together to make the answer."

He grinned. "Well, now we've got all the pieces, I guess. All we have to do is put them together!"

18

Jupiter Knows!

MRS GUNN fussed over the boys and the three men until they had eaten their dinner. Only then would she let them gather in the living-room to talk. Professor Shay began to pace the big room.

"We must solve the riddle, boys, or young Stebbins and that Java Jim will steal the treasure," the professor said. "It's clear now that they are working together."

"We haven't proved that, sir," Jupiter said thoughtfully. "But I agree that we must try to solve the riddle. We have all the pieces now—the journal trips and the letter—and I'm certain that old Angus planned a puzzle Laura could solve."

"Ay," Rory said, "I'll admit ye could be right —but it's a puzzle intended for one person a hundred years ago. Ye've tried, boys, but as I said from the start, it's no' solvable today!"

Cluny said hotly, "You sound like you don't want us to find the treasure, Rory!"

"Find it, then, and be hanged wi' ye!" Rory said sullenly.

Jupiter held the old letter of Angus Gunn's in his lap and opened the thin journal. Bob, Pete, and Cluny gathered round.

"We now have all four steps in old Angus's *last* course, the *days* that built Laura's surprise," Jupiter summarised. "What we must do now is try to see what they point to, and how they relate to the secret of Phantom Lake—that is, the legend of the phantom itself. And we must discover what a mirror has to do with the secret."

"Sure," Pete groaned. "That's all we have to do!"

Jupiter ignored the Second Investigator. "First, Angus went to Powder Gulch for sluice timber, supports, and miners. A big job, we decided, from the amount of food he bought.

"Second, he went to Cabrillo Island, made some proposal that the squire of the island agreed to, and came away with a *load* in his boat. He brought something *from* the island to here.

"Third, he bought ten two-hundred-pound, square-cut monument stones from the Ortega brothers and carted them here.

"Fourth, he bought something from Wright and Sons in Santa Barbara as a last touch to Laura's surprise. Something normally found on a ship, almost certainly, since that's all Wright and Sons sold in those days. Something with a brass plate with their name on it."

Jupiter stopped. Rory laughed where he sat near a front window.

"Ye put all that together," the Scotsman said, "and then ye chase a phantom that's no' even in this country! When ye catch your ghost, why, ye tell him to look in a mirror!"

"Gosh!" Bob flushed. "It does sound sort of—"

Mrs Gunn frowned at Rory and turned to Jupiter. "While you were all at the quarry, I looked and looked, but I couldn't find anything in the house with a Wright and Sons brass plate on it. I can't imagine what it would be."

Jupiter shook his head bleakly. "Whatever it was, I'm convinced that *all* the items that Angus bought have to add up to one thing. All of them go together, somehow, to make Laura's surprise. It has to do with what Angus loved at home, as the letter says. But," he finished lamely, "what could it be?"

"Something pretty big," Cluny said hopefully.

"What did Angus do with all that sluice timber and those men?" Professor Shay asked. "Where *is* all the timber?"

"And where did he put a ton of big stones?" Bob added. "I mean, ten monument stones are pretty hard to hide."

"Hey!" Pete cried. "What do miners do best? Jupe, you say always think of the most simple explanation. What a miner does best is—dig! They dug a big hole, used the sluice timber for supports and the big stones, too! Maybe an underground room!"

Professor Shay stopped pacing. "A big hole? In the ground?"

"Why not?" Pete insisted. "That'd be a good place to hide a treasure. Maybe Angus bought a brass handle from Wright and Sons, or a lantern for the hidden room!"

"But what would he have needed from Cabrillo Island?" Jupiter asked. "And I don't think a hidden underground room would have been much of a surprise for Laura. Remember, as far as we can tell, Angus planned the surprise first and added the treasure to it later."

Professor Shay hadn't moved since Pete suggested the big hole in the ground. Now he walked over to Rory near a front window.

"Have you ever seen any hint of such a hidden chamber, Mr McNab?" the professor said.

"No, I ha'n't," Rory snapped. "Poppycock!"

The professor looked out of a window at the small pond and dark trees. Suddenly he turned, his eyes bright.

"By George, I think Pete's right!" he cried. The Scottish Highlands are full of hidden caves and caverns. Mrs Gunn, the letter says to remember what Angus loved in Scotland, but you don't know what it was. What if it was—"

"A secret underground cave where they used to meet when they were younger!" Jupiter said. "Something only Laura would know!"

"Which Angus reproduced here," Professor Shay went on. "What he brought from Cabrillo Island could have been old Spanish furniture and rugs for the hidden cavern!"

"And a mirror, too!" Bob added.

Professor Shay nodded eagerly. "I think we have it, boys! It's obviously well hidden, and the entrance is probably covered over after a hundred years. But we'll find it! First thing tomorrow we'll start combing every inch of Phantom Lake!"

"Why not tonight!" Pete exclaimed. "We've got lights."

Professor Shay shook his head. "I'm sure we couldn't find much in the dark. Besides, we're all tired. We'll be more alert after a good night's sleep."

"The treasure won't run away, boys," Mrs Gunn said firmly. "Cluny, for one, is going to bed right now."

"But we know Stebbins is hanging around," Cluny protested, "and probably Java Jim, too!"

"I doubt they'll find much at night, either," Professor Shay said. "We'll have to risk it, but I don't believe it's much of a risk, boys."

They all nodded glumly. They knew the professor was right, but it would be a long night of waiting.

"I've got a hunch we won't sleep very well," said Pete.

"Then think about every possible way an underground chamber could be hidden," the professor said, "and tomorrow we'll all gather here and start searching."

"Ye'll search wi'out me," Rory said flatly. "I'll ha' no more o' this nonsense."

Professor Shay drove away in his station wagon. Pete, Bob, and Jupiter helped Hans load the pieces of furniture that Mrs Gunn had picked out for Uncle Titus, and then climbed into the back of the truck. The big Bavarian drove to the highway and turned towards Rocky Beach.

For a time, the boys rode in silence. Then Jupiter asked,

"How would someone mark an underground room, fellows?"

Pete thought. "Maybe pile up some of those big stones to look natural—but give Laura a clue?"

"Or," Bob said, "maybe plant a tree? A special tree like one they had at home in Scotland?"

"Yes," Jupiter said, "that's possible, Records."

"Maybe a mirror!" Pete exclaimed. "On the ground, or in a tree, and Laura would see it from some special spot!"

"From a window where she sat at home," Jupiter said. "Or from the top of the lodge's tower!"

"Gosh," Bob said, "any of those would work! I'll bet one of them is right, Jupe!"

Jupiter nodded, and stared out of the back of the truck at the first houses of Rocky Beach.

"Only one thing bothers me a little," the leader of the trio said slowly. "Old Angus's letter said to remember the secret of Phantom Lake—the phantom that watches for enemies coming up the lake. A hidden cavern doesn't seem to fit in with that legend."

"Maybe when we find the cavern we'll make the connection," Pete said.

"Yes, perhaps you're right, Second," Jupiter agreed.

Hans dropped Bob and Pete at their homes and drove on to the salvage yard. When Jupe got home, he was too excited to sleep right away. He had some hot chocolate and told Aunt Mathilda and Uncle Titus of the day's adventures. Uncle Titus hurried straight out to inspect what Mrs Gunn had sent him. Aunt Mathilda decided that a big hole hidden underground sounded exactly right to fit the riddle.

"You'll find it in the morning, I'm sure," she said. "Now I want you in bed, young man. You'll think much better when you're rested. Off with you!"

Jupiter lay awake for a long time watching the Christmas lights of Rocky Beach. But at last he fell asleep, still thinking of the hidden room, the big stones, the sluice timber, and Cabrillo Island where old Angus had gone to get . . .

Jupiter sat bolt upright in his bed!

He blinked, still half asleep. It was dark outside his window, but his clock showed that it was almost 8.00 a.m. Then he heard the drumming on the roof, and realised that it was raining hard outside.

But he didn't think now about the rain.

He sat there and stared at the wall. He knew the whole answer to Angus Gunn's riddle!

19

The Riddle is Solved

JUPITER DRESSED and called Bob and Pete. He told them to meet him at the salvage yard in fifteen minutes. He had the answer!

"I've been dumb," the stout leader of the trio moaned. "I should have seen it long ago. Hurry!"

He called Cluny at Phantom Lake.

"I think I know where the treasure is, Cluny," Jupiter declared to the sleepy boy on the other end of the phone. "Get a pick and shovel and your raincoat, and wait for us. Hans will drive us out."

He hurried downstairs to have a quick bowl of cereal. As he gulped his milk, the telephone rang. It was Professor Shay.

"Jupiter?" the professor said. "I've been lying awake in bed thinking about our hidden room, and I've had an idea of how old Angus could have marked it! The phantom—"

"There isn't any hidden room, Professor," Jupiter told him. "I'm certain I know the answer now!"

"What?" Professor Shay cried over the telephone. "Not a hidden room? Then . . . ? Tell me, Jupiter!"

"I'll tell you at the lake. Meet us there."

"I'll get dressed at once!" the professor said. Ten minutes later, The Three Investigators huddled in the rain in the salvage yard. Pete and Bob could barely contain themselves. When Hans arrived with the truck, they clambered into the covered back and faced Jupiter.

"What *is* the answer, First!" Bob demanded.

"Tell us!" Pete echoed.

"All right," Jupiter said, with a maddening grin. "I was asleep, and the hidden room theory was bothering me, and something Bob said when we rode home must have popped into my head. Then I saw the whole thing!"

Pete groaned in the bumping truck. "*What* did Bob say?"

"He said," Jupiter intoned solemnly with his love of drama, "that maybe old Angus planted a special tree at Phantom Lake. And that's exactly what Angus did!"

"A tree?" Pete gaped.

"Not a tree that he knew from Scotland, as Bob thought," Jupe went on, "but a tree that would make Laura think of home. He went to Cabrillo Island and bought one of those twisted cypress trees that look like phantoms! He planted a phantom at Phantom Lake!"

"Wow!" cried Bob. "All we have to do is find an old cypress out at Phantom Lake!"

"But," Pete objected, "where do we look? There's acres and acres of trees out there."

"The rest of the riddle tells us." Jupiter beamed. "Think of the steps to the puzzle again. First, the miners and the sluice timber from Powder Gulch. Pete was absolutely correct—miners *dig* best, and they did dig a big hole. And there is one vital fact about sluice timber we completely overlooked Why did old Angus have to have *sluice* timber? Not just planks, or mining timbers, but sluice timber?"

"Why, Jupe?" Pete sighed.

"Because sluice timber is specially cut and fitted to hold water!" Jupiter declared. "A sluice holds water *in*, but old Angus used it to hold water *out*!"

Bob stared. "Out of where, Jupe?"

"Out of the big, long hole he had the miners dig for him," Jupiter said. "He had to keep water out of the hole while it was being dug. Then he bought ten large stones to use as stepping stones. He got a cypress from Cabrillo Island. And what he bought at Wright and Sons was a ship's lantern!"

"The island in the pond!" Bob and Pete cried together.

"Exactly," Jupiter crowed. "Old Angus built that small island in Phantom Lake! That was Laura's surprise. Everyone thought old Angus *found* the pond with the island in it, just like home, but he didn't. He *built* the island!

"Originally there must have been a narrow peninsula jutting out into the pond. Angus built a barrier of sluice timber on each side, cut a channel across the peninsula, put the big stones in to be the Phantom's Steps, and let the water back in. He had an island then. He put a ship's lantern from Wright and Sons on a pole for a beacon, and planted a twisted cypress to recreate the legend of the phantom!

"He built a miniature replica of what he had *loved at home*—the view down the loch. That was his surprise present for Laura." Jupiter paused for breath. "Then, when the Captain of the *Argyll Queen* and his men appeared, Angus used his island as a hiding place for the treasure. He left the letter and the second journal as clues!"

Bob and Pete were silent in admiration of old Angus's clever riddle and Jupiter's solution of it.

"No one ever knew the island was man-made?" Bob said finally.

"No one besides Angus, except the miners who dug it," Jupiter said. "Miners in those days were mostly drifters, and even fugitives. By the time anyone started looking for the treasure, most of the diggers had probably gone away. Angus's family assumed that the island was natural, and never knew about the miners because they never read the second journal!"

"But we found it, and now we'll find the treasure!" Pete exclaimed.

"I'm certain of it," Jupiter declared.

Bob said, "One thing still confuses me, First. What did old Angus mean when he wrote about seeing the secret in a mirror?"

"Maybe the pond is like a mirror?" Pete suggested.

Jupiter said, "I think I can explain that, too. But first I want to go to the pond and—"

The truck had turned on to the side road to Phantom Lake some minutes earlier. Now Hans slammed on the brakes, throwing the boys backwards. They recovered, and jumped out. Hans was already out of the cab, hurrying forward.

They were at the last curve before the lodge, just out of sight of the house. Professor Shay's station wagon was parked on the gravel shoulder behind a grove of pines. The car's front door was open, and the professor himself sat on the edge of the front seat with Cluny bending over him!

"You are all right, Herr Professor?" Hans asked.

"I . . . I think so," Professor Shay said, feeling his jaw. He looked at the boys as they ran up. "It was Java Jim! I drove up just a few minutes ago and saw him on the road! I tried to apprehend him, but he attacked me and ran off into the trees!"

"Java Jim?" Jupiter cried. "Then we haven't a second to lose! Cluny, get the tools, quickly!"

20

The Phantom's Secret

MRS GUNN watched them go off through the rain towards the small pond, with Hans and Professor Shay carrying the tools.

"Be careful now," Cluny's mother called. "Try to keep dry."

The boys nodded, and hurried through the undergrowth to the edge of the pond. The Phantom's Steps gleamed wetly in the narrow channel. They jumped across the stones in single file and stood on the tiny pine-covered island. It was less than one hundred feet wide, with two small hills that reached up thirty or forty feet.

"The legend says that the phantom stands on a crag and watches down the loch for the Vikings," Jupiter said. "So we'll look for a twisted tree on the far side of the island on some high point!"

They circled the island to the far side, the rain dripping off their hats and coats and down their necks. They climbed up the slope that formed the tiny hill facing down the pond. The beacon was on the top, its lantern hanging against the pole. Pete inspected the lantern.

"Jupe was right!" the Second Investigator

exclaimed. "The brass plate's on the lantern—
'Wright and Sons'!"

"Look for the twisted cypress," Jupiter urged.

But there was no need to look far.

"There it is!" Professor Shay cried.

It stood not fifteen feet away from the beacon
—a small, twisted cypress just like those on Cabrillo
Island. In the rain it looked like a ghostly human
shape with a gnarled head and a long, skinny arm
pointing out towards the pond. Like a phantom
forever watching out to sea for the Vikings to
come again.

"Look," Pete said, pointing back towards the
lodge across old Angus's man-made channel.
"The cypress is completely hidden from the house
and shore by other, bigger trees. No wonder we
never noticed it."

Jupiter nodded. "It was probably clearly visible
when old Angus planted it here, but these dwarf
cypresses grow very slowly. It probably hasn't
grown a foot in the last hundred years, while the
other trees grew to hide it."

"Never mind about trees, First!" Pete declared.
"Let's start digging!"

Bob looked all round the cypress. "Java Jim
hasn't been here, Jupe. No signs of digging."

"Come on, Pete," Cluny urged, reaching to
take the pickaxe from Hans. "We'll dig all
round—"

"No," Jupiter said. "We won't dig here."

They all looked at him.

"But, the letter says remember the secret of

Phantom Lake," Professor Shay said. "That must mean look where the phantom is."

"It also says to *see the secret in a mirror*," Jupiter reminded them. "Angus was saying look at the phantom in a mirror."

"There's no mirrors round here, First," Pete objected.

"No, and Angus knew that," Jupiter agreed. "So he must have meant *as if* in a mirror. A mirror reverses things! So Angus meant us to reverse the phantom to find the treasure!"

He looked at the stunted old tree. "The phantom looks and points out to the pond. So we have to reverse it—and look back along the pointing arm the other way!"

Suiting action to words, Jupiter stood in front of the small cypress and stared back along the thin, armlike branch. Bob looked along the arm behind him.

"Gosh, I can't see much through this rain," Bob said. "It's too dark today."

Jupiter said, "Give me your flashlight, Cluny!"

Jupiter laid the large flashlight along the arm of the phantom tree and switched it on. The strong beam shone through the rain—and fell on a flat, open area of thick brush. Jupiter started.

"Hurry, fellows!" he cried.

They all scrambled down the slope of the beacon hill and ran to the flat area. Overgrown with heavy brush, unmarked in any way, there was no sign to indicate that treasure might be buried there. No sign—until now!

They all stared at the torn-up brush—and the gaping hole!

"It's gone!" Cluny cried.

"Someone guessed before you, Jupe!" Pete groaned.

Professor Shay bent down. He held up a brass button. "Java Jim! That's why he attacked me and ran! He has the treasure!"

"We must call the police!" Hans said.

They rushed back across the Phantom's Steps and up to the lodge. Jupiter asked Mrs Gunn to call Chief Reynolds of the Rocky Beach Police and tell him that The Three Investigators needed help! Stop Java Jim from escaping!

"We'll search where he attacked you, Professor Shay," Jupiter decided. "Maybe we can see where he went!"

Where the professor's car had pulled off the road just out of sight of the lodge, they began to search the ground with their flashlights. The gravel round the car revealed nothing. Professor Shay pointed to an open space a little way from the car. It was muddy, and boot tracks crossed it going straight towards the highway. The professor sighed.

"He must have had his car on the highway. He's gone, boys!"

Jupiter examined the boot tracks in the mud. "These are shallow tracks," he pointed out. "Was Java Jim empty-handed when he attacked you, Professor?"

"Yes, Jupiter. He must have had the treasure in

his car already, and have come back for something. I'm afraid he's escaped now."

"Perhaps," Jupiter said slowly as they walked back to Professor Shay's car. Suddenly, he looked round. "Where is Rory?"

"Rory?" Cluny said. "I haven't seen him all morning, Jupe. He likes to take early morning walks."

Jupiter's eyes flashed in the rain. "Cluny, you said Rory's only been here a year. Just how did he come here?"

"Wh-why," Cluny stammered, "he just turned up with a letter from people we know in Scotland, Jupe. He knew all about our family and old home!"

"Anyone could learn that!" Pete declared. "Jupe, you think Rory's working with Java Jim? Or maybe *is* Java Jim?"

"He's the same size," Jupiter exclaimed. "He tried to stop our looking for the treasure from the start. He was away from Phantom Lake both times Java Jim tried to get the journal from us, and he showed up awfully fast at the ghost town right after Java Jim ran away!"

Bob said, "He knew we were at that quarry because he took us there! He was the first one we told about the ton of stone from the Ortegas. He could have locked us in that shack and come back here to knock down the smokehouse—he didn't know yet that the stones were all big ones!"

"But, we all saw Stebbins at that shack," Professor Shay said.

"Yes!" Jupiter agreed, "but Stebbins tried the padlock on the door. He wouldn't have done that if he'd locked Bob and Pete in, he'd have known the door was locked. And . . ."

Jupiter thought a moment. "Fellows, when we chased the man after the shed burned, did any of us really *see* any man?"

The boys looked at each other. No one had!

"We chased because Rory said he saw Java Jim," Jupiter went on, "but I wonder if Rory saw anyone? If there was anyone?"

"You mean Rory set the fire in the shed?" Bob asked. "He just pretended to see Java Jim? Because he *is* Java Jim?"

Cluny said, "Professor Shay saw the man running away!"

"And thought it was Stebbins," Jupiter replied. "Professor, did you really see anyone after that fire, or just *think* you did?"

"Stebbins was on my mind," Professor Shay said slowly, "but now that you mention it, I don't think I really did see anyone! Rory said he saw Java Jim. I knew . . . I mean, I thought I saw Stebbins."

"Rory's the thief!" Pete yelped. "Rory's got the—!"

A voice boomed in the rain. "Rory's got what, eh?"

The Scotsman stood in the road glaring at them.

"Ulp!" Jupiter swallowed hard. He steadied himself with a hand on the hood of Professor

Shay's station wagon, and dropped his flashlight. He bent to get it.

"Hans!" Professor Shay snapped. "Take hold of Rory there!"

When Jupiter straightened up, there was an odd expression on his face. He touched Professor Shay's car again, puzzled.

"No," the leader of the Investigators said suddenly. "Not Rory, Hans. I was wrong!"

21

The Treasure of the "Argyll Queen"

HANS HESITATED in the rainy road, watching Jupiter.

"Stay near McNab, Hans!" Professor Shay ordered. "Jupiter, what are you talking about? You just proved Rory is guilty!"

"He locked us in the shack at the quarry, Jupe!" Pete said.

"He set fire to the shed and knocked down the smokehouse!" Bob exclaimed. "You proved it, First!"

Rory was suddenly pale. "What? Ye accuse me of—!"

"You will not move," Hans said stolidly, his hand on the Scotsman's arm.

Jupiter shook his head. "Rory burned the shed, locked up Bob and Pete, and searched the smokehouse. He tried to stop us getting to the treasure. But he's not Java Jim, and he doesn't have the treasure."

"You're saying it was Stebbins and Java Jim?" Professor Shay asked.

"Java Jim, yes," Jupiter agreed. "Not Stebbins. He doesn't want the treasure. I think, in a way, he's been trying to help. When he broke into

Headquarters, he didn't try to steal the journal and keep us from searching—he just photographed it. Most important, we've usually seen Stebbins only after Java Jim was near. He's been following Java Jim and us! In Santa Barbara I think he only wanted to talk, but we made him afraid of us. I believe Stebbins sent that boy to Hans to help us out of the barge, and at the quarry he was trying to *free* Bob and Pete."

"You're saying Java Jim was alone after all?" Pete asked.

"Yes and no, Second," Jupiter said quietly.

Cluny wondered, "What do you mean, Jupiter? How can he—?"

"Java Jim is an odd man," Jupiter went on. "He seems to be a stranger, yet he knows a lot about this area. He showed up at the salvage yard right after Bob had been to the Historical Society. He broke into the Society the day we went to Cabrillo Island, but why? He didn't go to the *Sun-Press* first for the old Santa Barbara records, the way we had to—he went directly to old Mr Widmer. How did he know about Mr Widmer's private morgue?"

"Gosh," Bob said. "That's right. How did Java know?"

"He knew about Mr Widmer, Bob, because he's an expert on the history of our area!" Jupiter said, and now he looked at Professor Shay. "Rory wasn't the only one who appeared at the ghost town soon after Java Jim had run away—Professor Shay did! The professor is an expert on local history, and he *is* Java Jim, and he stole the treasure this morning!"

Professor Shay laughed in the rain. "Ridiculous, Jupiter! I'm not offended, my boy, but you're quite wrong. Why, I'm much too small to be that ruffian."

"No, sir, you're just thinner. A heavy pea-jacket fixed that."

"And just how did I steal the treasure this morning when I was at home in bed?"

"Last evening," Jupiter explained, "when Pete suggested the hole in the ground, you saw the truth before I did. During the night you came back and found the treasure, probably using a flashlight on the cypress branch just as I did. It was morning before you had dug up the treasure and carried it off. You heard the telephone ring in the lodge. To be sure the call wasn't dangerous to you, you slipped up and listened.

"You heard Cluny say we had the answer and were coming here. If you just ran, and we found the empty hole, we might suspect you later. But if you pretended that the mythical Java Jim had the treasure, and had escaped, then no one would ever suspect you. The police would go on looking for Java Jim!

"So you sneaked into the lodge, called me to pretend you were at home, and then went out to wait for us. You made those boot tracks yourself, and faked the attack by Java Jim."

Everyone was watching Professor Shay now.

Far off the siren of a police car was coming along the highway.

"Do you expect to prove all that, boy?" Professor Shay smiled.

"Yes, sir. Because you made a big mistake," Jupiter replied. "You said you were at home at eight o'clock this morning, and drove up here just before we came. It's been raining hard, though, since long before eight."

"Raining?" Professor Shay laughed. "I fail to see—"

"The ground is *dry* under your station wagon," Jupiter said simply. "And your car engine is cold. You had to have been up here long before eight o'clock."

With a cry of rage, Professor Shay turned and ran up the road towards the highway. The siren of a police car came down the road. Shay darted off towards the dark trees—and a thin shadow sprang from the wet bushes and leaped on him! There was a tangle of arms and legs, and the police car skidded to a stop. Two policemen jumped out and grabbed Professor Shay and his attacker.

As the boys, Hans, and Rory ran up, Chief Reynolds was looking puzzled. The chief was staring at Shay and—Stebbins!

"What's going on here, boys?" the chief demanded. "Is that young man fighting with Professor Shay the thief? Is that Stebbins?"

"I'm Stebbins," the wild-haired young man cried, "but I'm no thief! Shay is!"

"He's right, Chief," Jupiter said. "Professor Shay is the thief!" He explained all he had deduced. "I suspect that Stebbins never was a thief. I think he discovered that Professor Shay was after the treasure some time ago, so the professor had him sent to prison on a false charge!"

"It's true!" Stebbins nodded. "When I got out on parole, I came back here to watch Professor Shay and prove my innocence!"

Chief Reynolds looked severely at Professor Shay. "If you have the treasure, Professor, I suggest you tell us where it is right now. It will go easier for you in the long run."

Professor Shay shrugged. "Very well. Jupiter has beaten me. The back seat of my car is hollow, it's all under there."

Two policemen removed the back seat. They took out a pea-jacket, sailor's cap, muddy boots, heavy trousers—and a rubber mask of Java Jim's face with black beard, scars and all!

"He just pulled it over his whole head," Chief Reynolds said. "With the cap, pea-jacket, and disguised voice—he was Java Jim!"

But no one listened to the chief. They were all staring at the glittering mass under the hollow seat. There were rings, bracelets, necklaces, jewelled daggers and boxes, and hundreds of gold coins. The hoard stolen by East Indian pirates from countless ships and towns!

"Wow!" Pete breathed. "It must be worth millions!"

"Fantastic," Chief Reynolds said.

"I cannae believe it!" Rory said with wonder.

Professor Shay suddenly wailed, "It's mine, you hear? I'm not the thief—old Angus was the thief! He stole it from my ancestor! I'm a descendant of the Captain of the *Argyll Queen*!"

"That is a matter for the courts," Chief Reynolds said sternly. "After a hundred years, I doubt if you can prove your claim. Your Captain stole it, too—from the pirates. And *they* stole it in the first place. I'd say it belongs to Mrs Gunn now. As for not being a thief, perhaps not, but you could go to prison for breaking into houses and assaulting people!"

"And for framing Stebbins!" Bob suggested.

Chief Reynolds nodded. "Take the professor away, men!"

The professor was led away to the police car.

With Chief Reynolds, the others went to the house to get a chest for the treasure, which the chief had to hold as evidence for the time being. In the house, Cluny excitedly told Mrs Gunn all that had happened. Mrs Gunn was dazed.

"Then there is a treasure, and you found it?" she marvelled.

"And it's ours, Mum!" Cluny cried. "We're rich!"

Mrs Gunn smiled. "We'll have to see about that, but I thank you, boys. You are really fine detectives!"

The boys beamed happily.

"Jupe?" Pete said slowly. "I don't understand one thing. Professor Shay was Java Jim all along, and was after the treasure, but you said Rory did burn the shed and lock us in the quarry and try to stop us getting the treasure. Why did he do that?"

Jupiter grinned at Rory. "Well, I'm not sure, Second, but I think I could guess. I think Rory wants to marry Mrs Gunn, and he was afraid that if she were rich she wouldn't need him!"

Mrs Gunn looked at Rory in surprise. The craggy Scotsman turned beet red.

"Why, Rory," Mrs Gunn smiled. "I never guessed."

Everyone grinned at him. Rory blushed even more furiously.

22

Congratulations from Alfred Hitchcock

ALFRED HITCHCOCK sighed behind his desk. The
Three Investigators had once again come to his
office with an incredible tale.

"So after a hundred years there *was* a treasure,
and despite seemingly impossible difficulties you
found it!" the great motion-picture director said.
"Very well, I will write an introduction for this
case. Such bulldog tenacity must be honoured."

"Thank you, sir!" Bob and Pete cried.

"We've also been honoured with a few pieces
of the treasure," Jupe said. "Mrs Gunn gave them
to us as a reward. And she told us to keep the ring
we found in the secret compartment of the sea
chest. It turned out to be rather valuable. We
thought you might like to have this, sir." He held
out a jewelled Malay dagger. "For your collection.
A pirate weapon from the treasure."

"Thank you, Jupiter," Mr Hitchcock said. "But
I am, perhaps, even more interested in the story.
There could be a movie plot in it. Professor Shay
is a descendant of that nefarious Captain of the
Argyll Queen?"

"He is, sir," Jupiter replied. "He's a real histor-
ian, too, and was a sailor in his youth. It was his

interest in history and the sea that made him study his own family and discover the story of the treasure. He took the job here to look for the pirate hoard. Stebbins found out what he was doing, so he framed Stebbins and sent him to prison. When Mrs Gunn gave old Angus's first journal to the Historical Society, he did notice the missing two months between the end of the journal and old Angus's murder, as I suspected. He guessed there had to be a second journal somewhere.

"He broke into the Gunns' house repeatedly to search old Angus's things. He also traced what Mrs Gunn had sold. When he missed getting the chest in San Francisco, he came to the roadside museum where he ran into us. Mr Acres, the museum owner, knew him already, and Shay didn't want anyone to suspect he was after the treasure, so he used the Java Jim disguise. He invented Java Jim in the first place to keep everyone from guessing he wanted the treasure.

"After he joined with us in the search, he wanted to prove there was a Java Jim, so he cooked up that story of Java Jim breaking into the Historical Society. That was a mistake, because the moment I guessed Shay could be the thief, the story was an obvious lie. Java Jim had no real reason to break into the Society."

"Ah, the criminal mind," Mr Hitchcock said. "Always trying to be too clever, going too far."

"He's not really a criminal, sir," Bob said. "He just got carried away by greed. He says he's sorry now. Mrs Gunn has decided that he does have a real claim to the treasure, so she's giving him a third. He's going to use it for his defence, and give most of it to the Historical Society for exhibition."

"Mrs Gunn is a most generous lady," the famous director observed. "Perhaps Professor Shay can reform. He will go to prison?"

"Mrs Gunn won't prosecute him, and neither will we," Jupiter said. "There's no proof he broke into the Gunn house. However, he'll stand trial for his worst crime—the perjury and criminal fraud in accusing Stebbins and sending him to jail."

Mr Hitchcock nodded solemnly. "Young Stebbins was simply following the professor to try to establish his own innocence?"

"Yes, sir," Pete agreed. "And he was desperately trying to find out how much Shay knew. He saw Shay as Java Jim run from the salvage yard with the oilskin cover, and later saw Java throw it away as empty. It made him realise there *was* a second journal, and he didn't know then that we had it. So he went to the lodge to search. Rory saw him and chased him."

"Later," Hitchcock deduced, "Stebbins saw you boys with the journal and photographed it so he could know what was going on. He really wanted to help, but he was afraid no one would believe him against Professor Shay."

"Yes, sir!" Bob exclaimed. "He was afraid we'd believe anything Professor Shay told us. So he just followed us all, hoping to find some evidence against Shay and helping us out of tight spots along the way."

"He's been completely exonerated," Jupiter added. "The Historical Society gave him his job back!"

"Excellent!" Mr Hitchcock boomed. "And what of the romantic Rory?"

"Well"—Jupiter smiled—"he admits he wants to marry Mrs Gunn. He tried to stop us only because he was afraid she wouldn't marry a poor man if she were rich."

"And what does the lady say to the idea of marriage?"

"She says she'll think about it," Pete replied with a grin.

"Ah, then she *will* marry Rory," the famous director said. "Wonderful work, lads. I congratulate you."

Mr Hitchcock stood up to end the interview, and then eyed Jupiter quizzically. "Your reasoning was excellent, Jupiter. However, it strikes me that there could have been another explanation for the dry ground under Professor Shay's car—that a real Java Jim had parked there before Shay, perhaps. And car engines can cool rapidly in rainy weather."

"That's true," Jupiter conceded. "But when I guessed that Professor Shay *was* Java Jim, I remembered a worse mistake he made."

Mr Hitchcock frowned. "What worse mistake, young man?"

"When Rory set fire to the shed," Jupiter explained, "he faked seeing Java Jim. But Professor Shay insisted he saw Stebbins running away. He hadn't seen anyone, of course, but he got into a terrible argument with Rory. He argued so hard because—"

"He *knew* Rory couldn't have seen Java Jim," Mr Hitchcock finished. "Because he was Java Jim himself! Thunderation!"

"Yes, sir." Jupiter smiled. "And he almost made the same slip moments before I saw the dry ground under his car. He *was* Java Jim."

As the boys left, Mr Hitchcock found himself sighing. He felt almost sorry for any criminal who had to face Jupiter Jones!

CAPTAIN ARMADA

has a whole shipload of exciting books for you

Armadas are chosen by children all over the world. They're designed to fit your pocket, and your pocket money too. They're colourful, gay, and there are hundreds of titles to choose from. Armada has something for everyone:

Mystery and adventure series to collect, with favourite characters and authors – like Alfred Hitchcock and The Three Investigators. The Hardy Boys. Young detective Nancy Drew. The intrepid Lone Piners. Biggles. The rascally William – and others.

Hair-raising spinechillers – ghost, monster and science fiction stories. Super craft books. Fascinating quiz and puzzle books. Lots of hilarious fun books. Many famous children's stories. Thrilling pony adventures. Popular school stories – and many more exciting titles which will all look wonderful on your bookshelf.

You can build up your own Armada collection – and new Armadas are published every month, so look out for the latest additions to the Captain's cargo.

If you'd like a complete, up-to-date list of Armada books, send a stamped, self-addressed envelope to:

Armada Books,
14 St James's Place,
London SW1A 1PF